A Groom for Ruby

Laura Ashwood

Anchored Soul Publishing

A Groom for Ruby by Laura Ashwood

Scriptures quoted from the King James Holy Bible.
Cover Design by EDH Professionals

Get A Free Book!

You're just a moment away from:

* A FREE book

* VIP notice of sales and freebies

* Author happenings

* Great recipes

* Exclusive giveaways

* Special bonus content

* First peek at new covers and titles

Just scan the QR code to sign up for Laura's newsletter, or visit www.lauraashwood.com!

Also by Laura Ashwood

Contemporary

Royally Unexpected

A Little Something Sweet

One Sweet Christmas

Women's Fiction

Summer at Bluefin Bay

Historical

A Groom for Ruby

LAURA ASHWOOD

A Groom for Violet

A Groom By Surprise

Courting Danger

Always to you, Rod, for putting up with me when I am frantically trying to meet a deadline and listening to me cry over my characters. I love you and couldn't imagine life without you.

To our children and grandchildren...you are my joy, my hope and my life. I love you.

For I the Lord thy God will hold thy right hand, saying unto thee, Fear not; I will help thee.

~ Isaiah 41:13

Contents

Chapter One

♥

November, 1878 - Last Chance, Nebraska

Ruby Fulton slowly stirred the small pot of oatmeal with one hand and pulled her threadbare shawl tighter around her shoulders with the other. She could hear the wind howling outside and the heat from the cook stove brought little comfort to the drafty house. It would only get colder as winter approached. Ruby's shoulders slumped as she thought about everything that needed to be done. Cyrus hadn't gotten around to taking care of any of the winter chores before he'd left with the hunting

1

group that never returned.

Ruby shuddered thinking about it. The men had only been gone for a couple of days when the temperature suddenly plummeted. Thunder and lightning filled the skies and seemingly out of nowhere, a blizzard began to rage. The snow and wind continued for two days straight, dropping nearly four feet of snow on the ground. Ruby managed to save her flock of chickens by bringing them into the house with her, something she'd never dare to do if Cyrus had been home. Once the snow stopped, she frantically cleaned the mess they'd made in the small house. It wasn't until Sheriff Applebee stopped by the farm a couple of days later that she heard how many people perished in the blizzard.

With no sign of Cyrus and eggs piling up, she finally decided to make a trip into town. Mr. Talley at the mercantile regularly bought eggs from them, but Cyrus usually insisted on taking them to town by himself. He allowed her to go with him to church once a month, but said that any more than that wasn't necessary. Ruby suspected it had more to do with his proclivity to sleep in than anything.

While in town, she'd heard talk about the missing hunting party, but Pastor Collins had convinced the townsfolk to wait a few more days for them to make their way home before sending out a search party. Heather Barnes, the butcher's wife, was handing out smoked meat and Ruby gratefully took a sack. Cyrus hadn't done any hunting that fall, and their food store for the winter was far less than they'd need. While she'd gotten resourceful at making what little food they had stretch, she was more concerned than ever about how they'd make it through another harsh Nebraska winter.

When she returned home from town that day, she prayed fervently that Cyrus would not return from the hunting trip. Ruby had come to Last Chance five years earlier as a mail order bride, much like many of the other women in town. She'd been abandoned as

3

a young child, and only had vague recollections of someone that may or may not have been her mother. Somehow, she'd ended up in an orphanage in St. Louis, although she wasn't sure if that was where she was born. It was at the suggestion of one of the nuns there that she answered Cyrus's advertisement.

Ruby had high hopes of improving her station in life, but quickly learned that life with Cyrus Fulton was no improvement. He was a lazy man, and after several years had passed and she produced no heir for him, he became violent. She'd become adept at hiding or explaining most of the bruises over the years, but the pity she saw reflected in the eyes of the women in town shamed her to her core.

Not quite two weeks later, the second blizzard struck. This one came during the night. Ruby heard the wind pick up with the same eerie sound as it had when the first blizzard came. Again, she ran to the barn and brought her flock of chickens into the house. So many people lost livestock during the first storm, she knew she'd be able to sell her eggs and perhaps buy some dry goods with the money before Cyrus came back. She didn't know what he did with the egg money, but suspected it was spent at the saloon in town.

Once that storm passed and she'd managed a second trip into town, she learned that not only had all of the men in the hunting party been killed, but the group of men that had gone to retrieve their bodies had likely died too. Mrs. Talley told her that Pastor Collins preached that God was angry and was punishing the town. Ruby was overcome with guilt. This was her fault. God was angry with her. She had prayed Cyrus wouldn't return and as a result, none of the men would return. The oatmeal blurred as tears filled her eyes.

"I'm hungry, Miss Ruby," a small voice interrupted Ruby's thoughts.

She hastily wiped her cheeks and turned to face the young boy, who looked back at her with earnest eyes. "It's almost ready, Everett. Have you washed your hands?"

"Yes, Miss Ruby."

"All right then, why don't you set the table and by the time you're done, this will be ready."

He nodded and quietly did as she bid. The boy was always hungry, although by looking at his small frame, you'd never know it. Gideon and Ida Henzel owned the property adjacent to hers, and Everett was their young son. Gideon ran the sawmill, which was located on the large creek that ran through his property. They were an older couple, and while Ruby didn't know much about them, she had gleaned through bits and pieces of what Cyrus told her that Everett had been an unexpectedly late addition to their family. His birth had been quite difficult and Ida never fully recovered. Gideon blamed the child, and Ruby suspected the six years Everett had been alive had not been easy ones for him.

Gideon had gone with the hunting party, and

Ruby would never forget the haunted look on the little boy's face when he showed up at her door a couple of days after the second blizzard asking her to help him wake his momma. She'd ran with him the half mile back to their farm, but it was too late. Mrs. Henzel was gone. Ruby wasn't sure what had happened, but suspected when Ida had learned Gideon wasn't coming back, she had simply given up.

She'd bundled Everett up in clothing she found in the Henzel's house and walked with him to town to see Mr. Blanchard, the undertaker. Mr. Blanchard had dark circles under his eyes and looked completely overwhelmed. When she told him about Mrs. Henzel and asked what she should do with Everett, he told her to leave him at the diner. Hollie Dawson was taking in some of the orphans, and perhaps would have room for him, unless of course, she wanted to take him in herself. He wasn't aware of any family the Henzel's had in the area, but perhaps Pastor Collins, or Faith, who was now operating the post office, would know more.

Ruby had looked down at Everett's sad little face and her heart wrenched. She would provide a home for the little boy as long as he needed one. Vowing to have a conversation with Faith next time she came to town, they made a quick stop at the mercantile where Mrs. Talley gave Everett two gumdrops, and Ruby bought a bit of sugar with some of her egg money. She could tell Mrs. Talley wanted to ask her about the child, but was grateful when she didn't. She wasn't used to being in town and felt intimidated by most of the townsfolk.

They stopped back at the Henzel's on their way home from town that day. Ruby collected the one horse and cow that hadn't perished in the blizzard, along with the few articles of clothing Everett had, and the unlikely foursome made their way home. While Ruby managed to save her chickens, the small amount of livestock they owned perished in the blizzards. She had gratefully accepted responsibility of the Henzel's horse and cow until someone came along to claim Everett.

Ruby pushed the memories aside and pulled the pot off the stove. She scooped the steaming oatmeal into the bowls Everett had set on the table. Everett stared at the bowl with a longing in his eyes, but he made no move to pick up his spoon. Ruby knew he was waiting for her to let him know it was okay for him to eat it, and she was filled with a profound sadness for the little boy. On a whim, she reached into the small cabinet next to the dry sink and pulled out a small bag of sugar and the dish of butter. She watched Everett's eyes grow large as she placed a small pat of butter and a little sprinkle of sugar on his oatmeal.

"Go ahead and eat, Everett, before it gets cold," she smiled at the boy.

Everett picked up his spoon and a hint of a smile crossed his lips. "Thank you, Miss Ruby."

Ruby's heart swelled. It was the first time she'd seen anything that resembled a smile on his small face since he'd come to stay with her. She sat across from him and ate her plain oatmeal, letting it fill her with its warmth. The wind continued to howl outside, making the blankets she had tacked over the windows flap slightly and every now and then a little puff of snow would come through the walls where the chinking needed repair. Another thing Cyrus hadn't gotten around to before he'd left on the hunting trip. Ruby thought about all the work that needed to be done before the coldest part of winter came and set her spoon on the table. She was no longer hungry. Everett had just spooned the last of his oatmeal into his mouth and she pushed her bowl towards him.

"Can you do me a favor and finish mine?" she asked. "I'm plum filled up."

The boy nodded and pulled her bowl in front of him, eagerly digging his spoon into what remained of her breakfast, while Ruby tried to figure out what she was going to do. Mrs. Talley told her about the ad the women from town placed, looking for grooms to come to town, mostly at Pastor Collins' insistence. The last thing she wanted was another husband, but she knew she couldn't manage all of the repairs on her own and she didn't have anywhere else to go. She closed her eyes and rubbed her forehead. She got herself into this situation, it would be up to her to get herself back out.

"Miss Ruby, are you feeling poorly?"

Ruby opened her eyes and met Everett's concerned gaze. "No, Everett, I'm fine. Why do you ask?"

"Momma would close her eyes and rub her head just like that, and then she'd have to lay down for a long time. Only last time, she didn't get back up."

Ruby felt the back of her throat grow tight as Everett's pale brown eyes filled with tears. She walked around the table and pulled him into her arms, but released him when she felt him stiffen. He wiped his eyes with his small fists and the sorrow she'd seen on his face was quickly replaced with the blank expression he usually wore. She had always wanted a family, with lots of noisy children, but was relieved when she was unable to get pregnant with Cyrus's child. She didn't want to bring a child into their home to suffer at his heavy hand. But now, having Everett to care for, Ruby realized she didn't know the first thing about raising children and felt horribly inadequate. What should she do, for example, when Everett woke in the night, screaming in terror? She had no idea, but she resolved to be patient with him and let him come to her on his own time.

She watched as a shiver ran through Everett's slim shoulders. In an effort to make the rapidly dwindling woodpile last longer, Ruby had been putting a minimal amount of wood in the cook stove. But knew she'd need to come up with a solution.

Ruby quickly did their dishes and added one more small piece of wood to the fire. Everett had moved to the pallet she'd made for him on the floor next to the cook stove and huddled under his blanket. She'd given him the nice thick quilt she'd been gifted by Altar Pennington when she moved to Last Chance. Cyrus hadn't wanted her to accept it, saying they didn't need charity, but Ruby took it anyway. That was before she understood the cost of defying his wishes. It had become her most precious possession, reminding her that even in the worst situation there was kindness and beauty in the world.

She stared at the colorful pattern on the quilt for a moment, when an idea came to her. "Everett, bundle up, we're going to town."

Chapter Two

♥

November, 1878 - Dodge City, Kansas

Cullen Parker listened to Jim Morgan run through the plan while dread grew in the pit of his stomach. He knew coming to Dodge City with his brothers to meet up with the Morgans had been a bad idea, but his options had been limited. Dodge City had a wild and wicked reputation and was the last place he should be but his oldest brother, Frank, assured him it would be worth his time. He should have known better. He had just wanted to meet back up with his brothers and start his life over, but not this way.

"We'll start a fire on the track here," Jim said, and pointed to a spot on a crudely drawn map he had sprawled out on the rough-hewn table. He moved his finger to a different spot. "We can wait in this row of trees. When the train stops for the fire, we'll come up on it near the front."

"No," Warren Morgan broke in, shaking his head. He took a long pull of the amber colored liquid from the bottle he was holding and leaned back in his chair so far its front legs lifted off the floor. Cullen had never met the Morgan brothers, but it was obvious that while Jim did most of the talking, Warren was the smarter of the two.

"Can't use fire," Warren continued.

"Worked just fine before," Jim countered and grabbed the bottle from Warren's hands. He took a long drink and slammed the bottle on the table causing a bit of the liquid inside to slosh onto the map.

Warren reached for the bottle, the legs of his chair settling back in place with a thud. "Unless we put an entire tree on the track, that train ain't likely going to stop for no fire. We need to pull a rail."

"Pull a rail?" Cullen's younger brother, Ben asked.

"Remove part of the track," Warren said, taking another pull from the bottle.

"Why would you want to do that?"

Cullen groaned inwardly. Their father had always said Ben was a simpleton that asked too many questions. His willingness to follow orders, along with his considerable size and strength, made him an asset in many other ways though. The Morgans had built quite a reputation and Cullen knew Frank had ridden with them down to Lincoln County earlier in the year to ride with the Regulators after their brother, Virgil Morgan, had been killed. They were well known for their hair-trigger tempers. He watched as Warren looked Ben up and down, clearly sizing him up, and brought his hand down to rest on his thigh, closer to his gun.

Warren took another pull from the bottle and wiped his mouth with the back of his hand. "It'll derail the train. Gives us plenty of time to hit the express car."

Ben's mouth hung open while he processed that information, and Cullen said a quick prayer that he wouldn't ask any more questions.

Warren ran his finger along the line on the map that represented the train track and stopped at a curve. "If we pull a rail just after this curve, the engine man won't see it in time to brake. Train will come off the tracks for sure. Jim and I can get the money out of the express car, and the rest of you can get what you can from the passengers. We'll meet back here after and divvy it up."

"Not so fast," Frank cut in, his eyes narrowed into slits. "There's supposed to be a lot of money on that train. Ain't no way you both," he gestured to Warren and Jim, "are goin' in there alone."

Jim curled his lip. "You sayin' you don't trust us?"

"I'm sayin' you can hit the passenger cars with Cullen and Ben. I'll go with Warren in the express car."

The two men stared at each other for a long moment. Warren finally grunted his approval, and Cullen moved his arm back onto the table.

"We'll ride over there at first light and check the track. The train is supposed to come through at 11. Don't want to pull the track too soon, but from this point," he pointed to a bluff near the curve of the track on the map, "we can see it coming."

Cullen didn't like this. He'd done plenty of things he wasn't proud of, but he'd never put anyone's life in danger but his own. He knew his brothers wouldn't be quick to pull their guns, but a lot had changed since he'd been in prison and he didn't trust the Morgans. Getting locked up for robbing a stagecoach or stealing a horse was one thing, but they'd hang for sure if people were killed while they robbed a train.

Cullen was no stranger to life on the wrong side of the law. His father, Lewis Parker, was a gambler that always seemed to be on the run from someone. Cullen was born in New York, but had lived in Indiana, Kansas and Colorado Territory before his family settled down in Missouri. It was there that the sins of Lewis's past finally caught up with him and he was gunned down during a card game when he'd been caught with an ace up his sleeve. Frank had been fifteen at the time, Ben was thirteen and Cullen just eight. His mother, Adeline, had her hands full with the three rowdy boys and they often ran unchecked. Frank and Ben were expelled from school after they started it on fire, and were regularly brought home by the sheriff for stealing from the mercantile. Cullen usually tagged along with his brothers and even though he rarely participated in their criminal acts, he was given the same reputation as them.

Adeline contracted tuberculosis and died when Cullen was twelve. His brothers joined the Confederacy with some of their friends and went off to fight in the War Between the States. Cullen was sent to live with an uncle in Kansas. His aunt and uncle had a brood of their own they could barely take care of and they looked at Cullen as more of a nuisance than anything. But he learned valuable carpenter and wood working skills while he lived there. When he was sixteen his brothers returned from the war. They were headed west to make their fortune in California and Cullen followed.

Once in California, they discovered that there was no quick fortune to be made. Frank met up with a friend from the war who told him about the success Jesse James had robbing banks back in Missouri. After scouting several banks, they determined the risk was too great and decided to rob a stagecoach, bringing Ben and Cullen in to help. Wells Fargo coaches carried the famed green treasure boxes, which contained gold dust, gold bars, and gold coins, among other items of value, and they usually didn't have passengers. While the shotgun messengers hired to guard the coaches were crack shots, the group successfully robbed three of them. During the course of those robberies, not one person was shot nor were any passengers robbed.

It was during the fourth attempt that things went bad. Cullen hadn't wanted to do it. He'd never felt right about it in the first place. Besides, he'd saved more than enough money and gold to buy some cattle and settle down. But Frank talked him into it. Told him he'd heard there were two green treasure boxes on this coach. He promised it would be the last time. Cullen never found out if there were two green boxes or not because not only were there shotgun messengers on the coach, but several more that rode about a half mile behind the coach. They had just gotten the coach stopped when the guards on horses came up on them and gunfire ensued. Frank and Ben managed to get away, but Frank's friend was killed. It wasn't until later that Cullen found out that Ben had also been shot, but managed to recover from his wounds.

Cullen, however, was captured. He hadn't fired back, which saved him from the gallows, and he served four years out of a six-year sentence at San Quentin for robbery. He was pardoned upon release and vowed he'd never do anything to get himself put in prison again. He'd heard talk in San Quentin about gold being discovered in Dakota Territory and that's where he went. He settled in a mining camp in Deadwood Gulch, but despite some success in panning, the growing town of Deadwood was rife with crime and he went back to Missouri in search of his family.

Upon locating them, Cullen was disheartened to learn his brothers were still up to no good. As he listened to the Morgans outline their cockeyed plan to rob a train, he knew for certain that he wanted no part of this kind of life. He remained quiet while the plan was agreed on. Later that night, after he was sure everyone was asleep, he slipped out and quietly saddled his horse, grateful the sounds of the nearby saloon masked any noise he made. He pulled the collar up on his coat and headed north.

Just before he'd left Deadwood earlier that year, he'd heard talk of a mine being built just south of there in a town called Lead, where a huge gold deposit had been found. The Homestake Mine was supposed to be a big operation and Cullen was sure he'd be able to get a job there. He had no desire to stay in Kansas or Missouri, and was washing his hands clean of his brothers. He still had a stash of gold nuggets that would be more than enough to set him up once he arrived back in the Black Hills.

Cullen rode into Sidney, Nebraska cold, weary and hungry. He stopped at the livery and made sure Ghost, his appaloosa mare, was settled and fed, giving the stable boy an extra dime to brush her down. There was a restaurant just down the street from the livery and Cullen walked toward it, passing a busy saloon on the way. The sounds of music and laughter drifted out of the door as he walked past, but he had no desire to go inside. He just wanted to fill his belly and get a room at the hotel for the night.

The restaurant was nearly full, but Cullen spied an empty table near the back. He could feel several eyes on him as he made his way to the table, but didn't give it any mind. It was nice having a clean conscience and not having to worry about watching his back. A stout woman with red cheeks and kind eyes, wearing a brown dress and stained white apron, stopped at his table. She carried a pot of coffee and placed a tin cup on the table in front of him, filling it when he gave a nod of his head. Cullen gave her his order and sipped on his coffee while he waited. His stomach rumbled loudly when she returned with a plate heaped high with mashed potatoes and a thick steak, and she chuckled at him.

"You just passing through?" she asked, setting the

steaming plate in front of him. "I don't recognize you, not that I should," she chuckled again. "Most folks don't stay."

Cullen nodded, he wasn't up for small talk, but didn't want to be rude. "Heading north."

She lifted her eyebrows. "Oh, are you one of those grooms?"

Cullen frowned. "Grooms?"

"You know, heading to Last Chance. We've had a few of them catch the stagecoach here and head that way. Shame what happened."

Cullen had no idea what she was talking about, but it piqued his interest. "What happened?"

The woman gave a quick glance around the room before she returned her gaze to his. "The blizzards, of course."

Cullen furrowed his brow and shook his head, still not understanding. He knew there were a couple of bad blizzards in September, he'd just missed one on his way to Missouri, but wasn't sure what that had to do with grooms.

"The town's menfolk were apparently on a hunt when the blizzards came back in September," she lowered her head and her eyes filled with sadness. "Killed them all, it did. I heard the women put an advertisement in the paper for mail order grooms. Can you imagine? A town with no men?" she shook her head. "Figured if you're heading north this time of year, must be because you're one of them grooms."

Cullen shook his head. "No, I'm heading to Dakota Territory."

She nodded and waved at a couple of men who had just sat down at a nearby table before turning back to Cullen. "That's a shame, you'd make a fine husband for some woman," she gave him a wink and sauntered off.

Cullen cut into his steak and took a bite, savoring the rich flavor. His thoughts wandered to what the waitress had said. *A town with no men. What had she said the name of the town was? Last Chance?* There'd bound to be jobs in a town where the menfolk had been killed. He had no interest in getting married, but maybe he could find a job and someplace to stay until spring, then continue to Dakota Territory. Plus, there was something about that name that called to him. *Last Chance.* By the time he finished his plate, he'd decided that is what he would do. If he couldn't find work, he'd just continue on the Sidney-Deadwood Trail until he reached Lead.

Two days later, Cullen and Ghost rode into Last Chance. The town was larger than he'd expected, but he noticed most of the businesses he passed were closed. This made him even more optimistic about being able to find work. The mercantile was open and he tied Ghost to the post in front of the store. He held the door open as two women exited the store, staring curiously at him, and he could feel his face and neck grow warm.

He stepped inside and looked around. The store carried an impressive variety of items, and he selected a pouch of dried meat. A woman with a young girl clinging to her skirt smiled shyly at him before taking her purchases to the counter. Cullen wandered through the aisles, taking note of several items he'd return for if he were able to stay in the town. He made his way to the counter where an older gentleman with a full, dark mustache greeted him. At the end of the counter, a woman that Cullen assumed was the shopkeeper's wife stood talking quietly to another woman wearing a thick felt coat.

He pulled a coin out of his pocket and handed it to the shopkeeper. "Any work around here?"

The man eyed him carefully before responding. "There is a board outside the butcher shop. Might be something posted there." He slid a glance at his wife before handing Cullen his change.

"Much obliged," Cullen nodded. He turned toward the women and tipped his hat before walking out of the store. He glanced down the street but didn't see a butcher shop, so he climbed back in his saddle and rode toward the livery. He could see more shops down that road and it wasn't long before he saw the butcher shop. He slid off Ghost and walked up to the wooden board that was nailed to the side of the building. Several small pieces of paper were attached to it, some were too weathered and worn to read, but one in particular caught his eye. It looked as though it had been placed there recently.

Wanted: honest and sober man to do repairs on farm for room and board. See R. Fulton. 1 mile west of church. Painted star on barn.

It was exactly what he was looking for.

Chapter Three

♥

Ruby hefted the heavy ax over her head and closed her eyes as she brought it down on the small log, neatly splitting it in half. It was the last log on the pile. She rested the ax against the side of the barn and lifted her hands to inspect them. They were red and sore, and she could see blisters forming on her palms, but they weren't bleeding and for that Ruby was grateful. She gathered the small pile and carried it into the cabin, placing it in the wood box next to the stove. It wasn't enough to even fill it halfway and there was no more.

She shrugged out of her worn coat and hung it

on the peg behind the door and sighed. It had been several days since she and Everett made the trip into town where she had placed a help wanted note on the board outside the butcher shop. There had been no response thus far. Ruby eyed the table. If she didn't come up with a solution soon, she'd have to start burning the furniture.

Everett sat on his pallet on the floor, the pink tip of his tongue sticking out as he concentrated on forming numbers on his slate. He was such a quiet boy, and Ruby couldn't help but wonder if he had always been that quiet or if it was because of the shock of losing his parents. As she watched him, a thought suddenly occurred to her.

"Everett, is there a woodpile at your house?"

The boy nodded his head without looking up.

Ruby chewed on her bottom lip for just a moment, wondering if what she was thinking was a good idea. Surely it wouldn't be wrong to use the wood, seeing as how Everett was now staying with her and no one else was using it, would it? At this point, it was the best option she had.

"Everett," she crouched next to his pallet so she could look him in the eyes. "I'd like to go to your house to get some of the wood your pa cut."

Everett's pale brown eyes lifted and met hers. "Can I get my top?"

Ruby's heart fell. He hadn't mentioned he had any toys, and she hadn't thought to look for any when they made the brief stop there to get his clothing. "Of course you can," she smiled as she fought back tears. "Along with anything else you want."

They stopped in the barn to get the horse. Their wagon was too large for one horse to pull, but Ruby hoped the Henzel place would have something she could use in order to get some of the wood home. She slipped a rope onto the horse's halter, and they made their way toward the Henzel's house. The sun was shining high in the sky and it reflected brightly off the snow. While the air was crisp, it was not particularly cold and it felt good to be out of the confines of the small cabin. Even Everett's mood seemed to brighten some as he walked alongside her.

As they approached the house and silent mill, Ruby could see a very large pile of wood, stacked neatly under a lean-to next to the barn and she felt lighter. There was more than enough wood to last through the rest of the winter, she just needed to find a way to get it back to her house. She slid open one of the barn doors and was delighted to see a sled inside. Hanging next to it on a hook was a harness and reins for a single horse. She studied them for a moment before lifting them down and taking them outside where Everett waited with the horse.

She'd watched Cyrus hitch their horses up many times, but had never done it herself. However, this harness seemed much simpler than the one they had, and she was confident she'd be able to manage it. The horse stood patiently while she fumbled with traces and buckles until she had it situated properly. Then she went back into the barn, attached a thick rope to the front of the sled and pulled. It scarcely moved. She wrapped the rope around one of her hands and let it slide over her shoulder as she pulled again, heaving all of her weight forward. This time it moved a couple of inches.

"Miss Ruby, why don't you bring Buckshot in here and hook him up?" Everett's small voice stopped Ruby cold. All at once, she felt both incredibly relieved as well as incredibly foolish. She let the rope fall and turned to face the small child who was, at that moment, clearly more clever than she.

"Everett, that is a wonderful idea. Thank you for thinking of it. I don't know what I would do without you," she smiled gratefully at the boy, whose face shone with pride. Several minutes later she led Buckshot and the sled out of the barn, and brought them to a stop next to the woodpile. She tied the horse to the post of the lean-to and smiled triumphantly at Everett, who had been watching intently.

"Can I get my top now?" he asked, pointing at the house.

She glanced at the quiet house. As uncomfortable as it would feel to go inside, she had to remember that this had been his home and he had every right to be there. As his guardian, that meant she did too. At least that's what she told herself as she nodded her head. She followed Everett into the small room behind the large fireplace that held his bed, and where they'd gotten his clothes. Ruby wished they could bring his bed to her house, but there was no room in the tiny home. She could, however, bring the blanket and pillow from his bed.

"Everett, would you like to bring your pillow home with us?"

He looked at her with wide eyes and smiled. "Yes, Miss Ruby, and my blanket too?"

She returned the smile. "Your blanket too."

She helped him gather the bedding and set it on the table while she glanced around the tidy house.

She saw a container of coffee, along with several other dry goods on a shelf next to the dry sink. She only hesitated for a few seconds before she placed them on the table too. The food would spoil if it was left here, and there was precious little food left at her house. She ran her hand along the top of the large cook stove and wondered what it would be like to use such a fine appliance. The words of Exodus filled her mind, *thou shalt not covet anything that is thy neighbor's* and she reminded herself to be grateful for the stove she had.

The toe of her shoe bumped into something on the floor and she looked down. A small ring was attached to one of the boards and it looked as though there was a door in the floor. She slid a glance to Everett.

"It's the cellar," he shrugged. "I don't like it down there. It's dark and there are spiders," he made a face.

Ruby shuddered, she didn't like spiders either, but a cellar could mean more food. She pulled the ring and the door lifted easily, revealing a narrow staircase. She turned back to the dry sink, looking for matches to light the lantern that sat on the kitchen table.

"They're up there," Everett pointed to the top of the warming cabinet on the cook stove.

Ruby looked and sure enough, there was a box of matches. She turned to Everett. "How did you know that's what I was looking for?"

"Ma always took the lantern with her down there, so I figured you'd want to too," he said. "That way you can watch for spiders and stuff."

"Thank you, Everett. That was very helpful," she gave the boy a smile before striking the match and lighting the lantern. She slowly went down the stairs, half expecting to encounter layers of spider webs, based on Everett's opinion of the cellar. The room was fairly large and while it smelled musty, there were no cobwebs to be found, at least none that she could see from the bottom of the stairs. What she could see, however, were rows of shelves that were lined with jars and jars of canned food. In one corner were several barrels that, upon inspection, were full of a variety of salt-cured meat and fish. Ruby could have cried. *Thank you, Lord, for providing this bounty.* She also said a quick thank you to Ida, God rest her soul.

"Everett," she called. "Come and help me carry some of these jars upstairs please."

A shadow crossed the floor and his small face appeared at the top of the stairs, his eyes wide with worry. "It's scary down there."

"I'll be right here with you, and I promise there are no spiders," she beckoned him with her hand and he reluctantly descended the stairs.

They took only a small number of jars, as Ruby had little space to store them. She was also afraid of breaking the precious cargo. The wood salt barrels were too heavy for her to move, and she didn't have anything to carry the meat in, so she left them and would bring something with her next time she came over. *Next time.* Her heart grew heavy at the thought.

She still felt like she was pilfering off the misfortune of others.

She closed the cellar door and carefully wrapped the jars in Everett's blanket. A large basket was on the floor near the door and she filled it with the dry goods she'd taken out of the cabinet. Remembering why they were in the house in the first place, she looked at Everett.

"Did you find your top?"

A wide grin spread across his face and he nodded. He lifted his arm and in the palm of his hand, he proudly displayed an empty wooden spool with a carved piece of wood sticking out of each end.

"That's a lovely top," she exclaimed, and marveled at the boy's joy over such a small object. They gathered their treasures and left the house, carefully closing the door behind them. Ruby arranged the blanket with the jars, and the basket in the front corner of the sled and began to load it with wood. Everett joined her, and before too long they had enough wood in the sled to last them for several days. She hadn't wanted to overfill the sled and strain the horse, not to mention her arms were already sore from chopping wood and she would have to unload the sled once they returned to her house.

She had Everett climb onto the small wood pile in the sled and made a kissing sound to urge Buckshot forward. She walked beside the horse and by the time they reached her small farm, the sun was starting to sink on the horizon, casting a pinkish-orange hue across the western sky. She brought the sled to a stop near the barn and unhitched Buckshot and got him settled before gathering the items that needed to go into the house.

Everett followed her inside and she carefully unwrapped the jars, letting out a sigh of relief when she saw that none of them had broken. She placed the food reverently into her dry sink and spread the blanket on Everett's pallet. He lay on his stomach on the floor in front of the cook stove happily spinning his top. Not wanting to interrupt his fun with his newly-returned toy, Ruby stepped outside to unload the sled.

She had just pulled the door shut behind her when she caught movement out of the corner of her eye. There was a man she'd never seen before taking the wood out of the sled and stacking it neatly against the barn wall. Ruby flung the door back open and raced inside in the house, slamming the door shut behind her. *Who was he and why was he there?* She gave a panicked glance around the room and grabbed the shotgun off the rack on the wall. Cyrus had taken his rifle with him on the hunting trip, but thankfully he'd left the shotgun behind.

"Everett, stay put. No matter what happens, you don't leave this house, you understand?"

The boy looked at her with terror in his brown eyes and nodded. Ruby's heart was pounding so loud she couldn't tell if he'd said anything or simply nodded. She said a quick prayer, swallowed hard and stepped outside, pulling the door tightly shut behind her.

The man, who must have heard the commotion in the house, stopped what he was doing and was watching her intently. A white horse was tethered to the broken fence next to the barn, and Ruby assumed it belonged to him. She didn't see anyone else, but she couldn't be sure there wasn't someone hiding in the barn. She turned her attention back to the man. He wore a long brown duster and had a brown leather hat pulled low over his eyes. He wasn't an overly large man, but he could easily overpower her.

She raised the gun to her shoulder and rested her cheek on the cool barrel. Her hands were shaking so badly, she could barely hold it steady. "Take one more step and you're a dead man," she called in a voice that sounded much braver than she felt. She'd never shot a gun in her life, but he didn't know that. Her breath caught in her throat and she heard no other sounds but the crunch of snow under his boot as he took a cautious step backwards and raised his hands, his fingers splayed wide.

"What's your business here?" her already sore arms were now beginning to shake with the weight of the gun and she didn't know how much longer she'd be able to hold it.

"I'm looking for R. Fulton," he called and slowly lowered one hand into the pocket of his jacket.

He's going for a gun! Ruby pulled the trigger and the gun roared, creating a small cloud of smoke. The barrel slammed into her shoulder and jerked her backward, nearly causing her to fall but somehow she managed to stay on her feet. The man fell to the ground and Ruby clenched her jaw as her stomach dropped to her feet. Her fingers went numb and a strange buzzing sound filled her head. *She'd killed him.*

She held her breath and took a tentative step forward. The man began to move and she raised the gun despite the screaming pain in her shoulder. Then she saw the large hole in the side of the barn. She hadn't hit him at all. A mixture of relief and terror coursed through her and she tightened her grip on the gun.

He once again lifted his hands, empty fingers splayed on one side and a familiar-looking piece of paper clenched in the fist of the other.

"Don't shoot!" he called. "I'm looking for R. Fulton," he gave the paper in his hand a slight wave. "I'm here about the job."

Chapter Four

♥

Cullen waved the job posting in the air as he stared down the barrel of a shotgun in very unstable hands. He'd been in plenty of dangerous situations before, but it never occurred to him he'd go out at the hands of a woman. He'd known right away he was at the right place by the dilapidated condition of the buildings, including the small house. He was quite certain that if the roof didn't already leak, it would soon. But it was the magnificent star painted on the side of the barn that drew him in like a promise. A promise he could feel in his soul. He couldn't explain it if he tried, but he somehow knew he belonged here. If he wasn't killed first.

"Are you R. Fulton?" he called, still holding his hands in the air. The woman holding the gun narrowed her eyes at him suspiciously. She was small, and he could see by the quiver in her arms that she wouldn't be able to hold the gun much longer. Her brown hair, which was almost the same color as her worn dress, had at one time been pulled back into a tight knot at the back of her head but strands had broken free and flew raggedly about her pale face. From this distance, she looked neither intimidating nor particularly beautiful, which was fine with Cullen. He didn't need a woman to distract him, he just wanted a job to get him through the winter.

"Who are you?"

Cullen took a tentative step forward. "My name's Cullen Parker, ma'am," he said in the calmest tone he could manage, considering the circumstances. Although if the first shot was any indication of her skill with a gun, he didn't think he was in any real danger of being hurt, but he didn't care to be staring down the business end of a gun. "I'm here about the job. Is there an R. Fulton here?"

She lowered the gun to her slim waist and her cheeks flooded with color. He took another step forward and saw both fear and strength in her eyes. "I'm Ruby Fulton," she lifted her chin in an attempt to look confident, but her shaking hands and wary expression told a different story. The door to the house remained closed and by the condition of the property Cullen guessed she was here by herself, which would explain why there was now a fresh hole in the side of the barn.

"Ma'am," Cullen slowly lowered his hands to his sides. "I came to talk to you about the job, but if you no longer need the help," he glanced at the broken fence and shrugged, "I'll just be on my way. I'm sorry to have troubled you." He turned and walked toward Ghost. He figured if she needed the help, she'd stop him, but he wasn't about to cause her more fear than he already had.

"Wait," her voice held a note of panic. "Don't leave yet."

Cullen stopped and turned around, holding back a satisfied smile. "I'll stay if you stop pointing that gun at me."

She glanced down and shifted the weapon, so its barrel now rested against her shoulder. "I'm terribly sorry about that. I wasn't expecting..." she stammered, "you startled me. I didn't hurt you, did I?"

"No," he smiled. "I can't say the same for the barn though. I hope you didn't have any livestock on the other side of that wall."

Her cheeks flushed again and a hint of a smile played on her lips. "No, they are on the far end. Would you like to come inside? I can make a pot of coffee and we can talk about the job."

"I'd like that," he followed her into the small but tidy house. Cullen shrugged out of his coat but watched her place the gun back in the rack on the wall before he turned his back to hang it on one of the pegs behind the door. He removed his hat and hung it on a second peg. It was then he noticed the small boy on a makeshift bed on the floor, huddled against the wall near the cook stove.

It wasn't much warmer inside the house than it was outside and it didn't take Cullen very long to figure out why. The chinking in the walls was in bad need of repair, and while he'd seen the closed wooden shutters on the windows from outside, once inside he saw that instead of glass, they consisted merely of folded quilts tacked to the wall. There was no fireplace, only a small cook stove.

His jaw clenched, and he pressed his lips together. *What kind of man lets a woman and child live like this?* Then he remembered to reserve judgment until he knew the whole story. There could be a legitimate reason. As Cullen watched Ruby put a pot of coffee on the stove, a number of different scenarios ran through his mind, but none of them made sense. *If she had been alone for some time, why wouldn't the townsfolk help her? And if she hadn't, where was her husband now? Was he one of the men that died in the blizzard the waitress told him about?* He felt strangely protective of this woman he'd just met. Maybe it was the way she reminded him of a wounded animal, the way she watched him. Like she was ready to bare her claws at any moment.

Cullen turned his attention to the boy, who stared at him with an empty expression. "Who do we have here? You're no bigger than a mite, are you?"

The boy scrambled to his feet and hid in the folds of Ruby's dress. She reached her hand back and tenderly touched the youngster's head before taking two tin cups out of a small cabinet and placing them on the table. She settled the boy back on the floor and gave him a slate and small piece of chalk. He'd never seen such a quiet child.

"Why don't you sit," she stood and gestured toward one of the two chairs in the room. Cullen frowned and rubbed his hand along his jaw. Whatever had happened here, it hadn't been good. He pulled the chair nearest him out and sat down. Ruby used a folded cloth to take the coffee pot off the stove and she poured some of the hot liquid in each cup, before sitting down in the chair across from him.

He picked up the cup and sniffed, expecting it to smell like boiled water. Instead, a strong, rich aroma filled his nose. He took a sip, letting the smooth, full-bodied liquid slide down his throat and warm his belly. He closed his eyes for a moment, savoring the flavor. It was the best coffee he'd ever tasted.

"Is it all right?" Her voice was laced with concern and he opened his eyes and met her nervous gaze. "I can make another pot if it's not good." She slid her chair back as if to stand.

Cullen blinked. Once. Twice. "No, it's fine. It's actually wonderful. Really, please stay seated."

Ruby settled back into the chair and wrapped her hands around her cup. A little grimace of pain flitted across her features and she moved her hands to her lap. If he hadn't been watching her, he might not have noticed, but now he found himself wondering what had caused it.

She cleared her throat and fidgeted in her chair. "As you can see, there are a number of repairs that need to be done here."

Cullen nodded. "Where's Mr. Fulton?"

Ruby's face turned pale and he instantly regretted asking the question.

"Dead," she said simply, offering no further explanation. Her face showed no emotion, and he wondered how much experience she had hiding what she felt.

"I don't have the means to do them myself," her gaze shifted to her mug and she ran her teeth over her bottom lip. "I...," she glanced at the child, "we need some help. I can't afford to pay you," her eyes lifted and met his. They were a rich brown, the color of fine whiskey, and had a haunted, almost hollow look to them. While he guessed she was several years younger than he was, it looked like she too had lived more than her share of life.

"But I can provide room and board. I know it's not much," she continued, and her gaze shifted to her cup, which she had yet to touch.

"I'd be grateful for the work, and the shelter, ma'am," he took another sip of the delicious coffee. "I can get the repairs done and anything else you might need help with, and be on my way come spring."

She lifted her gaze and smiled at him, and when she did, the air went out of him. Her whole face lit up when she smiled and he forced himself to look away. There was something about her that he couldn't put his finger on, but he had time to figure out what it was.

"Thank you," she said, then worry crossed her face once more. "There isn't much room in the house, and it's...well...it's..." She glanced at the corner of the room where a blanket had been hung in front of what Cullen assumed was her bed.

"I'll be fine in the barn, ma'am," he assured her. He'd certainly slept in worse places and wasn't about to compromise her reputation.

"Thank you," she said and rose to her feet. "There's plenty of hay in the loft, and I can give you extra blankets." She disappeared behind the curtain and returned a minute later with two thick quilts draped over her arm.

Cullen drank the last of his coffee and stood. He ran his fingers through his hair, then reached for his hat. He placed it on his head and slipped into his coat. Ruby handed him the quilts and quickly stepped away.

"If you want to get yourself and your horse settled, I'll put supper on," she reached up and grabbed a lantern off a small shelf and handed it to him. "Should be ready in about an hour. You'll find feed for the horse in the barn as well, and an empty stall next to our horse, Buckshot."

"Thank you, Mrs. Fulton," he tipped his hat and pretended not to notice her wince when he'd said her name. He stepped out into the dark night and walked toward the barn. He hadn't been sure what had drawn him to Last Chance, but he knew without hesitation that he was exactly where he needed to be.

Chapter Five

♥

Ruby opened a jar of peaches that she'd brought from Henzel's cellar and put together a quick cobbler. It was a special treat to celebrate her good fortune today. Not only had she solved her food and wood supply problem, but Cullen Parker had showed up and would get her house repaired and weatherproofed. Even after she'd almost killed him. Her face flushed hot as she gave a quick prayer of gratitude for her bad aim.

She glanced at the chair where he'd been sitting, and thought about how very different his presence in this house seemed than Cyrus's, even in the short time he'd been inside. She'd always felt like she was about to be pricked with a pin when Cyrus was around. It was impossible to determine when his mood would change, and he would become angry or aggressive, even over the smallest things. Ruby shook her head and pushed those thoughts back to the far corners of her mind where they couldn't hurt her.

She turned to check on Everett. He was sitting on his pallet with his back against the wall and his slate balanced on his knees. His little brows furrowed as he concentrated on whatever he was working on. She'd been somewhat surprised when he'd hidden in her skirts when Mr. Parker spoke to him, but could understand his fears. It made her feel good that he was now comfortable enough to come to her when he was scared. Her mind drifted back to her childhood at the orphanage in St. Louis. *Not every child was that lucky.* She returned her attention to the little boy.

"What are you writing, Everett?" she asked in a soft voice.

He looked up and turned the slate around to show her. Everett had drawn a small tree next to a very large house. On the other side of the house were two figures, one slightly taller than the other.

"It's me and you," he pointed to the figures with his small hand and smiled shyly at her.

Ruby pressed a hand to her chest and felt her heart flutter. Her throat grew tight and her eyes burned as she tried to blink back tears. "It's a fine drawing, Everett. I love it." She crouched down beside the pallet to get a closer look at the slate. He had drawn something next to the figures, but she was unable to make out what it was. She pointed to it. "What's this?"

"It's a dog," he said. "Isaac and Eliza have a dog. He walks to school with us sometimes."

"His name is Racer, right?" Ruby had seen the black and white dog a couple of times when the Gruby children had come to pick up Everett on their way to school. They lived just over the hill from her farm, and had walked with him before the storms had changed everything. Now, they picked him up at her farm, rather than his former house. The arrangement worked well.

Everett nodded. "Yes, he's so fast. Do you think that's why they call him Racer?" His pale brown eyes searched hers for confirmation.

"I do. It's a clever name."

Everett turned the slate back around and studied his drawing. "I always wanted a dog of my own," he said in such a quiet voice, Ruby barely heard him.

"You know what?"

He looked back up at her, his eyes wide with interest. "What?"

"I always wanted a dog too," she confided.

"Did your pa tell you dogs were stupid too?"

"No...I just wasn't allowed to have one." She didn't want to tell him she had no father. None that she had ever known anyways. Pets of any kind were forbidden at the orphanage where she was raised, and she had been too afraid to ask Cyrus for one. She brushed a stray hair off Everett's forehead and her heart hurt for the child. She'd ask Mr. Talley about it next time she was in town. Christmas was just around the corner and she would love nothing more than to surprise Everett with a dog of his own.

Her gaze shifted back to the drawing on his slate. She too loved to draw her dreams as a child. Now she drew on scraps of paper when she could, and hid them in the barn. Ruby made a mental note to see how much some parchment and a charcoal pencil would cost. She felt like she had found a kindred spirit in Everett, and wanted to encourage him to continue to dream.

"Is Mr. Parker going to stay with us?"

Everett's question took her off guard, but of course, the child would have been listening to their earlier conversation. "Yes, just for a while. He's going to help fix some of the broken things around here."

"It's awfully cold in the barn," Everett frowned.

"Maybe he could use one of my blankets."

Ruby pulled the boy into her arms and held him close. He stiffened at first but then let himself relax in her embrace. She kissed the top of his head. "You are such a good boy, Everett." The child had next to nothing, yet was willing to give away one of his few possessions to help a stranger. If she'd have been able to have a child, she'd want him to be just like Everett. *But you don't deserve a child*, she could hear Cyrus's voice boom. She closed her eyes and tried to block the painful memories that churned in her head.

"Miss Ruby, why are you crying?"

Ruby's eyes flew open and her gaze locked with Everett's. She hadn't felt him step away. She touched her cheek and her fingers came away wet. She hastily grabbed a corner of her skirt and wiped her face. "I'm sorry, Everett, I'm fine," she reassured the child, forcing her mouth to smile. "I gave Mr. Parker blankets, so you don't need to give him yours. But it was awfully nice of you to offer it."

Mr. Parker! He'd be returning for his meal any minute and she hadn't finished preparing it.

"Oh goodness, I have no time for wool gathering, I need to get supper finished." Ruby scrambled to her feet, and grabbed what was left of the salt pork out of the cabinet. She cut it into slices and put it in the pan to fry. While it was browning, she mixed the batter for corn cakes. She flipped the pork and while she waited for the other side to brown, she stepped behind the curtain. Cyrus had thought mirrors were only for the vain, but Ruby had a small hand mirror that she kept hidden in her drawer. She pulled it out and gasped when she saw her reflection. Her normally tight chignon had come loose and strands of hair had escaped everywhere. Ruby smoothed it back and hastily re-pinned it.

By the time she returned to the cook stove, the salt pork was just beginning to burn and she chastised herself for her vanity. She didn't know why it had mattered to her whether her hair was in place or not, she was a plain woman and quite certain Mr. Parker wouldn't see her as anything but plain.

There was a soft knock at the door and Ruby smoothed her skirt before going to open it.

"Evening, ma'am," Mr. Parker stood in the doorway with his hat in his hands, and she stepped aside to let him in. "Whatever you're cooking smells delicious."

"Thank you," she murmured. "It's almost ready." Heat flooded her cheeks and Ruby couldn't help but watch him as he took off his coat and hung it up. He was tall, but not overly so, and lean, but his shoulders were wide and looked muscular. His thick brown hair curled over his collar and when he turned around, she quickly averted her gaze, avoiding his eyes. Ruby had a strange feeling in her stomach, one she'd never felt before, and wondered if it had anything to do with the handsome man standing on the other side of the room. He crossed over to where Everett sat on his pallet, and Ruby watched them out of the corner of her eye while she made the corn cakes.

"What have you got there?" Mr. Parker asked Everett, whose hand was clenched in a tight fist.

Everett studied the man crouched in front of him for a long moment, then slowly uncurled his fingers, revealing his little top in the palm of his hand.

Ruby looked at the two of them and said a little prayer, thinking how blessed she was that she hadn't taken any of the letters that came to town.

Chapter Six

♥

Cullen walked around the farm and made a note of all the repairs that needed to be done. He was appalled at the condition of the outbuildings and most of all, the house. He set about repairing the chinking on the outside of the small house with bits of wood he found in the barn, hoping it would help abate at least some of the winter wind and cold. He wondered again what had drawn him to stop in Last Chance instead of just riding straight to Dakota Territory. He could have made it in a little better than a week. His mind wandered to the woman inside and her son, who had the same haunted look in his eyes as she did. Maybe it was some sort of penance for all the poor choices he'd made in his life.

He came around from the back of the house and stopped when he saw Mrs. Fulton and the boy hitching their horse to the sled he'd unloaded when he arrived. He watched her clip a rope to the horse's halter while her son climbed into the sled. She glanced at him and hesitated a moment. He noticed how worn her dark coat was and couldn't help but wonder if she was cold. She acknowledged him with a slight nod of her head and led the horse and sled down the road.

Cullen briefly wondered where she was going, and why she walked beside the horse, rather than ride it. *Not your concern*. He shrugged and went back into the barn to find more wood he could use for chinking. There weren't a lot of scraps, and he suspected she'd burned most of whatever scrap wood had been available. The small pile of wood he'd stacked against the barn would not last through the week, and he made plans to cut more later that day. Right now, he just wanted to find enough to finish chinking the outside of the house without having to use what was in the wood pile.

He glanced around the barn. It was disorderly, but the stalls were clean and there was a decent supply of hay and feed. A couple of hens wandered in through the open door and clucked softly at him. They stared up at him, cocking their heads from side to side as if trying to figure out what he was doing and who he was. He'd seen the small coop when he first rode up to the farm, and rebuilding it was another item on his ever-growing list. There would be no shortage of things for him to do while he was here.

Not finding what he was looking for, Cullen looked up at the hayloft. He had set up a bed of sorts in a large pile of hay that filled most of the loft, but hadn't checked to see what else might be up there. He climbed the ladder and looked around. There were a few chunks of wood scattered about under the small, dirty window in the gable wall. Cullen went to pick them up when something in the shadows of the far corner of the loft caught his eye. He walked over to see what it was and found a worn leather trunk, covered with a thick layer of dust. *What was that doing up here?*

Cullen leaned over to inspect it closer and noticed small fingerprints in the dust near the edge of the lid. The leather was scuffed and peeling and steel nail heads once created a pattern around the front and sides of the trunk, although very few remained intact. He knew he shouldn't open it, that it was wrong, but a whisper told him he needed to. The broken latch reinforced the whisper, and he gingerly lifted the lid. The trunk was nearly half-full of paper in many different shapes and sizes. But it wasn't the variety, or even the quantity of paper, that drew his attention. It was the drawings on them that mesmerized him.

He carefully lifted out one of the larger sheets and studied it. It was a pencil sketch of a woman gazing tenderly at an infant cradled in her arms. The detail in the woman's face was extraordinary. Cullen pored over the rest of the drawings in quiet amazement. Many of them were of a woman and an infant or child in various poses, but there were also incredible sketches of landscapes, flowers, and animals. Whoever had drawn them had an undeniable gift. *Could Mrs. Fulton have drawn these?* Cullen wasn't sure but he had a feeling there was a lot more to her than the quiet, withdrawn woman he'd seen thus far. There was something about her that intrigued him and made him want to get to know her better.

He returned all of the drawings to the trunk and carefully closed the lid. He wanted to finish the house before Mrs. Fulton came back from wherever she had gone.

With one final swing of the mallet, the last bit of chinking on the outside of the house was filled. He would still need to fill in the smaller gaps with clay, but it was a significant improvement already. The rhythm of approaching horse hooves drew his attention, and he watched as Ruby led the chestnut gelding toward the house. The boy sat high in the sled and Cullen squinted to see what he was sitting on. It was a pile of cut wood. *Had she cut that? She must have, where else would she have gotten it?* The muscles in his jaw tightened as they came to a stop next to the barn.

"What are you doing?" His eyes narrowed, and he strode toward her, his fingers curling at his sides. *He was supposed to cut and gather the wood, that is why she hired him. What kind of man would let a woman do a man's work? Her husband might have been that kind of man, but he most certainly was not.*

Cullen stopped next to the sled and pointed at the wood piled high inside. "Did you do this?"

Mrs. Fulton lifted her head, and Cullen watched the color drain from her face. She took a step backward and slid a quick glance at the boy.

"Everett, go in the house," she said in a shrill voice.

Cullen watched in bewilderment as the child glanced at him with wide, frightened eyes and then ran toward the house. He pushed his hat back and rubbed his forehead.

Mrs. Fulton flinched. She had her elbows pressed tightly against her sides and her eyes seemed overly bright. She opened her mouth as if to speak, but no words came out, and a faint line appeared between her eyebrows. She took another small step backwards, not taking her eyes off him for a moment.

Cullen's chest tightened and his throat grew thick. *She thought he was going to strike her.*

"I'm sorry," he stammered. His cheeks burned with shame. "I didn't mean to...," he trailed off, unsure what he could say to remedy the situation. His stomach churned in disgust and his shoulders slumped. *He'd never struck a woman in his life.*

"I...I just went to get some wood," she choked out and Cullen could see she was struggling not to cry, which only served to make him feel even worse.

He stared at the slight woman standing next to the sled, and it was then he noticed the dark shadows under her eyes. Deep brown eyes that stared back at him warily. Whatever she'd been through before he arrived had not been good. There was a certain strength about her, yet at the same time an almost childlike vulnerability, Cullen realized, feeling an odd tug at his heart. She clasped her hands together, and winced almost imperceptibly. Almost.

"May I see your hands?" He asked in as soft and gentle a tone as he could muster, and took a careful step toward her. Then another, and another until he was standing directly in front of her.

Her brows furrowed and she hesitated for a long moment before she slowly lifted her hands, her eyes remaining downcast. He took them in his own and gently turned them over. The palms of her hands were scraped nearly raw. Cullen recalled how she'd winced when she touched the hot cup of coffee and knew she'd brought the wood that he had stacked when he'd arrived. His hands were big, rough and calloused, whereas her hands were small and soft. She had long, graceful fingers and he couldn't help but wonder if they were responsible for the drawings he'd seen in the trunk. They looked like the sort of hands that should be drawing or caressing a child, he thought of the many illustrations he'd seen, not for cutting and hauling wood.

"Do you have any salve?"

Her gaze snapped up and surprise registered on her face.

"In the house," she said in a quiet voice.

They stood staring at each other, his fingers still wrapped around her hands. The world around them ceased to exist for the briefest moment, then she blinked and pulled her hands away. Her face flooded with color and she stepped back, tripping on a stray piece of wood. Cullen shot out a hand and steadied her. She gave him a tentative smile before turning toward the house.

They stepped inside and Mrs. Fulton lit the lantern on the table, illuminating the little boy who was curled up on the pallet, fast asleep. Cullen again thought about how quiet and subdued he was, especially for a child so young. His gaze shifted and he saw Mrs. Fulton struggling with the lid of a small jar of what he assumed was the salve he had asked her about.

"Let me get that for you," he stepped over to where she stood and took the jar from her. It opened easily in his hand and she reached to take it back. He pulled it away and motioned for her to sit at the table.

"Let me," Cullen said, and pulled the chair out for her.

She tilted her head and looked at him with an odd expression on her face, but sat down. He moved the other chair over and sat in front of her. He coated his finger with the salve and reached for her hand. She stiffened and shook her head.

"There's no need to do that, Mr. Parker," her

cheeks turned pink and she pulled her hand back. "I am capable of..."

Cullen gently grasped her hand and pulled it toward him. "Yes, I'm sure you are," he agreed and gingerly spread the ointment over her wounded palm. When he was done with that one, he reached for the other. She watched him in stunned silence.

"Your boy is sure quiet," Cullen remarked, screwing the lid back on the jar.

She looked at him blankly, then her eyes grew wide. "Oh no," she gave her head a slight shake. "He's not my son." Her gaze shifted to the child and she looked at him with the same tender expression he'd seen on the drawing of the woman and child.

Cullen frowned. "I don't understand."

Mrs. Fulton sighed and traced a scratch on the top of the table with her fingertip. She explained to him how Everett came to be in her care, while he listened intently.

"So, how long was he alone with her before he

came to get you?"

She shrugged, "I'm not really sure, but he has nightmares nearly every night."

That would explain the dark circles under her eyes. He shook his head in disbelief. "Where did they live? That must have been a long walk for such a young child."

"Their house is about halfway to town from here," she said. "Where the sawmill is. In fact, that's where I was today," she gave him a sheepish, almost apologetic smile. "There wasn't enough wood. Cyrus hadn't gotten around to cutting it before..." she shifted uncomfortably in her chair, "the storms. I thought maybe there would be some wood there, and because Everett is staying here..."

"You thought it would be all right to use it," he finished for her. Her eyes snapped to his and she looked at him with a mixture of regret and fear.

"Should I not have done that? I didn't mean to steal it," her chin quivered. "I just thought...," she trailed off and glanced at Everett, who rolled onto his back and let out a soft moan.

Cullen's throat grew tight and he ran his hand across his mouth. What this woman had been through in the last few months was more than he could imagine. "Mrs. Fulton, you didn't steal anything," he said. She looked up and relief spread across her face. "You are caring for their son. However...I must insist that from this point forward, you allow me to haul the wood."

Her cheeks flushed a bright pink and her smile lit up her face in a way that made her look beautiful in the glow of the lantern. Cullen felt that odd tug on his heart again.

"Thank you, Mr. Parker."

"Please, call me Cullen."

She nodded. "All right, Cullen, but you must then call me Ruby."

"All right, Ruby," he smiled, liking the way her name rolled off his tongue. It was going to be an interesting winter.

Chapter Seven

R uby inhaled deeply, she loved the crisp clean smell of winter air. The sun shone brightly in the sky and the temperature was pleasant enough that her worn wool coat kept her comfortably warm. She walked slowly to town, egg basket over her arm, thinking about everything that had transpired since the blizzards changed her life. A heaviness filled her heart. *Changed everyone's lives*. She couldn't help but wonder if she hadn't prayed so hard for Cyrus not to return, if the outcome would have been the same.

She walked past the church and stopped for a moment to gaze into the schoolyard. It was quiet, and she thought of Everett inside. He'd only recently returned and she hoped being around other children would help him. While the circumstances with which he came to stay with her were awful, she thanked God every day that he was in her life.

Ruby made her way down Main Street, past the mercantile, and came to stop in front of the post office. She'd been putting off this visit for weeks, but knew that she owed it to Everett to find out if he had other family. The idea of losing him now was almost more than she could bear. The quiet little boy had worked his way into her heart. She drew in a deep, steadying breath, and knocked on the door.

Faith Thornton opened the door. Her surprise at seeing Ruby on the other side of it was evident in the way her eyes widened. Ruby felt her face grow warm and wondered if she'd made a mistake by coming here.

"Ruby," Faith smiled warmly, "what a nice surprise to see you in town. Come in, please," she held the door open and stepped to the side to allow Ruby to come in.

Ruby hesitated for just a moment, then stepped inside. She took a quick glance around, trying not to stare. She'd never been in such a fine house. The sound of a fussing infant came from another room and Ruby froze. Faith must have noticed because she let out a little laugh.

"Altar is here with her twins," her brown eyes twinkled at Ruby, and she felt herself relax a bit. "You've got to see them," she took Ruby by the arm and led her into the sitting room. Altar looked up and a bright smile filled her face. She held a swaddled infant in her arms, and Ruby could see the other sleeping in a large basket next to her on the floor.

"Why Ruby Fulton, it's good to see you again," she said. She glanced at Faith and raised her eyebrows. "Ruby stopped by my house to see the twins the day Pastor Collins was there. Got herself quite a shock."

"That man," Faith exclaimed. "I know he's a man

of God, but the way he thinks he can..."

"Now Faith, don't say something you'll regret," Altar interrupted. "It worked out just fine for me," she winked at Ruby. "Wolfe is more than I could have asked for." The baby in her arms made a soft cooing sound. "Would you like to hold him?" Altar held the baby toward Ruby.

Her stomach tightened and she held her hands up. "Oh...no, I - I couldn't possibly...I've never..."

Altar stood and placed the babe in Ruby's arms. "Sure you can. This here is Omega," she said, then gave a quick nod to the babe in the basket, her long braids swaying over her shoulders. "That's Alpha."

She'd never held an infant before and was afraid if she moved, she'd drop him. Altar gently guided her toward the sofa and Ruby sat, feeling somewhat more at ease. She stared at the baby nestled in her arms. He had a perfect little nose and she couldn't help but smile as he opened his tiny, toothless mouth to yawn. She was amazed how something so small could be so perfect. He looked up at her with innocent, dark brown eyes and she just knew he would grow to be a very wise man. "He's perfect," she breathed.

"So, what brings you by, Ruby," Faith asked and Ruby's head snapped up. She'd been so lost in the moment, she'd nearly forgotten why she was there.

"Oh, yes," she swallowed. "I've taken in Everett Henzel."

"Oh yes," Faith nodded. "I heard about Ida. What a shame."

Ruby nodded. "Yes, well, ummm, Mr. Blanchard didn't know of any extended family, and suggested I check with you, being the post mistress now. I...I'd like to keep him, but know if there is other family..." A family. It was the one thing that Ruby had always wanted. A family of her own, but she wouldn't deny Everett the opportunity to stay with his family, if he had any.

Faith thought for a moment. "I don't believe they had any other relatives," she finally said.

Ruby bit back a smile.

"If I remember right, I heard Ida telling Mrs. Talley that when they first moved to Last Chance. And I know they have never received any mail from family," she continued. "I think it's wonderful that you took him in, the poor child."

"What do you mean?" Ruby couldn't help but ask.

"Well, it was really no secret that Mr. Henzel blamed the boy for Ida's...afflictions. He wasn't the most pleasant man in the first place, I remember Aaron saying he wished Gideon wasn't going on the hunt with them."

Ruby saw Faith's eyes cloud over and felt her stomach rise and the back of her throat grow tight. She had seen Faith and Aaron together in church, how happy and in love they were, and often wondered what it would be like to be loved like that. She couldn't imagine the loss Faith must feel.

The three women sat in awkward silence for a

moment, then Omega began to fuss. Ruby's heart pounded in her chest and she turned to Altar. "I'm sorry, I didn't mean...I don't know what..." She held the baby toward his mother who took him and held him against her shoulder. He stopped fussing immediately.

"It's all right, Ruby," Altar smiled. "He's just hungry is all."

Ruby let out a sigh of relief and stood. She still needed to go to the mercantile and didn't want to intrude on their visit any more than she already had.

"If you're wanting to keep Everett permanently," Faith said, "you should talk to Judge Bringegar."

"Thank you, Faith." She hadn't thought about what might be involved in being able to keep Everett permanently, but now that she knew it was an option, she wondered what it would cost to do so.

She took one more glance at Omega and Alpha, then said goodbye to Altar. Faith walked her to the door.

"Thank you for stopping by, Ruby. Please don't be a stranger," she smiled and waved as Ruby walked toward the street.

Ruby reflected on her visit, and how welcome the two women made her feel. She'd never really had an opportunity to make friends before. Children came and went on a regular basis at the orphanage, and Cyrus, well, Cyrus wouldn't allow her to have friends. She thought about Altar's twins and then about the beautiful quilt Altar had gifted her years back. *Perhaps she could find a gift to give back.* Her step lightened as she walked toward the mercantile.

The door opened, just as she was about to grasp the handle and Ruby gasped and stepped back as Altar's new husband, Wolfe, stepped out of the mercantile.

"Oh, sorry, Miss Ruby, I didn't mean to startle you," he said in a deep, low voice.

Ruby had never seen a man so tall in her life, and tried not to gawk as she had at his and Altar's wedding. Well, if you could call it a wedding, with her lying in bed just days after the twins were born. Ruby had never felt so out of place in her life as she had that day.

Wolfe held the door open so Ruby could enter the store.

"Thank you." She gave him a hesitant smile as she stepped past him. She placed the egg basket on the counter for Mr. Talley, and began looking around for something that might be a suitable gift.

"We've never gone through so much butterscotch as we have since he came to town," she heard Mrs. Talley say.

"I hear he's a fine blacksmith, and heaven knows we needed one" another voice said, and Ruby peered around a shelf to see who it belonged to. *Penelope Purcell*. Even Ruby had heard about how much she liked to gossip. She ignored the women and returned to browsing. A stack of parchment caught her eye and she suddenly had an idea.

Ruby stood at the counter and waited while Mr. Talley counted her eggs, and placed them into a different basket. She looked thoughtfully at the bolts of fabric behind the counter. "I'll take three yards of the blue cotton too," she said with a smile. She gazed at the blue fabric and knew it would make the perfect gift.

"Well, I think it's downright improper, especially in front of that child," she heard Mrs. Purcell say in a loud whisper and she froze. *Was she talking about her?* She knew she shouldn't eavesdrop, but found herself listening intently.

"She needs the help," Mrs. Talley whispered back. "He's only staying until spring."

They were talking about her! Ruby felt her face grow hot and she turned to Mr. Talley.

"The eggs looked really good today, Mrs. Fulton," he said in a loud voice, giving her a sympathetic look. "I subtracted the cost of paper and fabric, do you want me to credit your account for the difference?"

Her eyes burned and she tried to swallow the lump that had formed in the back of her throat. "Yes, please," she managed and placed the material and the parchment in her basket. She all but ran toward the door when a man stepped out from one of the aisles. Ruby nearly crashed into him, stopping just in time. Her gaze lifted and she found herself looking right into Pastor Collins' eyes.

Her stomach dropped to her feet and she took a step backward. She gripped the handle of her basket so tightly her fingers felt numb. She tried to go around him, but he stepped to the right and blocked her path.

"Mrs. Fulton, how wonderful to see you again," his lips curled into a grin that never reached his eyes. "I've been meaning to pay you a visit."

Ruby's heart was pounding so hard, she was sure he could hear it. She knew what would happen if he came out to the farm. Cullen would leave. She stared at a button on the preacher's coat, unable to meet his eyes, and held her breath.

"You can expect me midweek," he said and stepped aside.

Ruby slid past him without a word and ran out the door. She hurried down the street and didn't even pause to watch the children at play in the schoolyard. She just wanted to go home. With Cyrus gone, it now had some level of security that came with the familiarity of the house. And she knew Cullen would be there. Pastor Collins would run him off, she just knew it.

Tears swam in her eyes as she thought about Cullen having to leave. There was so much work that still needed to be done and, if she was to be honest with herself, she enjoyed his company. She recalled what the pastor had said to Altar about sin before he'd all but forced her to marry Wolfe. Cullen had plans to leave in the spring anyways, there was nothing to keep him in Last Chance.

Ruby took a deep breath, wiped her eyes, and

squared her shoulders. Cyrus Fulton hadn't broken her. Neither would this. She'd manage somehow, she always did.

Chapter Eight

♥

Cullen sat and watched Ruby carefully stitch a patch over a hole in Everett's shirt. When Everett had come home from school that day he'd been in tears. He and Ruby had both run to see what was wrong, and it had taken several minutes before they were able to understand what had happened. He had gotten the shirt caught on something at school and it tore a small hole in the back of the shirt. Cullen watched as Ruby took the child in her arms and consoled him, telling him it was all right and that he wasn't in trouble. He couldn't count how many shirts or pairs of pants he'd torn as a child, and had never given it any thought. His mother had simply mended them and that was that.

A heaviness came over him as he sipped his coffee and let his mind wander while he watched Ruby pull the needle in and out of the thin fabric.

Earlier in the week, Cullen had hitched both horses to the wagon he'd found in the barn, and drove to the Henzel place to get another load of wood. Ruby had explained how she'd come across the cellar, and after he assured her it was all right to use the food stored in it, she'd asked him to bring back one of the salt barrels of meat as well. The Henzel's home wasn't hard to find, and he was surprised he hadn't noticed the sawmill on his way to Ruby's farm the first day he'd been in town.

The mill was built next to a large creek and was larger than what he'd expected the small town to have. A large paddle wheel turned aimlessly as water rushed over it, and he saw a circular saw inside the mill house. He brought the wagon to a stop in front of the Henzel's house. It was well-built and considerably larger than the log home where Ruby lived. What struck him as odd though was the fact that there was no indication at all that a child had ever lived there.

"Penny for your thoughts," Ruby's soft voice broke through his rumination and he met her gaze.

He shifted in his seat and glanced at Everett, who was on his pallet, drawing on his slate. "I was just thinking he's lucky to have found you," he said quietly.

"I think I might be the lucky one," she brought the shirt up to her mouth where she used her teeth to sever the thread.

Cullen studied her face for a moment. Ever since she'd come back from her trip to town a couple days earlier, she'd been subdued. He wondered what happened, but couldn't bring himself to ask her. He was leaving in the spring, and he needed to remember that. He couldn't let himself get attached to her, or the child. It wasn't right.

Stay. It was as if someone had whispered the word inside his head, and an image of the sawmill ran through his mind. Surely he couldn't...no, he'd made his plans, and he would stick to them. He was just about to get up and head to the barn for the evening when Everett stood and walked over to the table. He stood there for a minute, his hands clasped tightly in front of him, while he shifted from one foot to another.

"Everett, what's wrong?" Ruby asked.

"Miss Ruby, I was just wondering what's Christmas?" he asked.

Cullen frowned. *What child didn't know about Christmas?*

"I heard some of the kids at school say it's coming," the young boy looked at Ruby with an anxious face. "Is it bad?"

Ruby slid a quick glance at him, her brows furrowing the tiniest bit, before turning to Everett. It felt like she had just shared a secret with him, and a strange warmth spread across his chest.

"No, Everett. Christmas isn't bad. In fact, it's the opposite of bad," she said in a gentle voice.

A look of relief spread across Everett's face. "When is it coming? Can we see it?"

Ruby's gaze shifted to him, and Cullen could see tears forming in her eyes. He glanced at Everett, who was looking up at Ruby with such hope in his eyes, he could feel his own eyes start to burn.

Ruby took a deep breath as if she were gathering her thoughts and rose to her feet. "Everett, bring the wood box over and sit down, I'll be right back," she disappeared behind the quilt that hid her sleeping area.

Everett pulled the wood box over and set it on its side. He'd been using it as a chair since Cullen's arrival. Cullen had asked Ruby about bringing the table and chairs from the Henzel's home over, but she wouldn't have it. It was one thing to take survival items, she'd told him, but something entirely different to take their furniture. He had reflected on that for a long time, and knew he'd be a better person for having known this woman.

Ruby came back to the table with a thick black leather-covered book in her hands. She sat and flipped through the book until she found what she was looking for.

"Christmas is when we celebrate Jesus's birthday," she said.

"Who's Jesus?"

"Jesus is God's son."

"Who is God?"

"Oh my, did your parents ever take you to church?"

"You mean the tall building with the cross that's by the school?"

Ruby nodded.

Everett shook his head, his brows furrowed.

"Oh my," Ruby said. "Let me see how I can explain this to you."

Cullen sat back in his chair and listened attentively while Ruby explained to Everett how God created everything, including him. She was patient when he asked questions, and answered them in such a simple way that he was sure Everett understood. Cullen's family hadn't been particularly religious, but his mother read the Bible out loud to them when he was a young boy. Somewhere along the way, he'd forgotten about it. He dropped his chin and stared at the table. *He'd have to fix that.*

"So Jesus is God's son, and Christmas is the day Jesus was born," Ruby said. "This is how it happened," she looked down and began to read. "And it came to pass in those days, that there went out a decree from Caesar Augustus that all the world should be taxed."

Cullen listened to her tell the story, and even though he'd heard it before, he was just as mesmerized as Everett. So much so, he'd let his coffee get cold.

"Do I have a birthday too?" Everett asked.

Cullen cringed inwardly. Ruby closed the Bible and placed it on the table, something in her expression had changed, but he wasn't sure what it was.

"Yes, you have a birthday too, Everett. Everybody has a birthday."

"Do you know when mine is?"

Cullen watched as Ruby finger-combed the boy's hair and placed her hands on his cheeks. "I'm not sure, Everett, but I'll find out."

"Thank you, Miss Ruby."

"All right, then, it's about time for you," she touched the tip of his nose with her finger, "to go to bed. Isaac and Eliza will be here before you know it to take you to school."

"Yes, Miss Ruby." He wrapped his arms around her neck and gave her a hug. He turned to Cullen and gave him a shy smile. "Good night, Mr. Parker."

"I should be going too," Cullen said, rising to his feet. "Good night, Everett."

Ruby's eyes met his and he could see a flash of anger in them. She held up her hand. "Cullen, wait," she stepped around the table and reached for her coat. "I need something from the barn, would you walk with me?"

"Of course," Cullen couldn't imagine what she could possibly need from the barn, but he took her coat from her and held it up so she could more easily slip it on. He took the lantern he'd been using off the hook and lit it.

"I'll be right back, Everett," Ruby said over her shoulder, and she followed him out the door.

They were about halfway to the barn when he stopped and turned to look at her. "You don't really need anything from the barn, do you?"

She shook her head. Her mouth was pressed into a thin line, and her fingers were curled into fists at her side. She looked at him for a moment, then started pacing back and forth in front of him. Cullen watched her, unsure what he should do or say. He finally decided to watch and wait. It seemed like the safest decision based on the ferocity of her expression.

She stopped and looked up at him. "How can a child not know what Christmas is?"

Cullen wasn't sure how to answer, so he said nothing. He watched with interest as she started pacing again. He'd never seen a woman so angry before, it was like she was so mad she didn't know what to do with herself. She stopped again and he tensed. While he knew she wasn't mad at him, he still wasn't sure what she was going to do. Bursting into tears was the last thing he expected.

"He d-didn't even know he had a birthday, Cullen," she cried. "Can you imagine? It's like he was invisible to them. What kind of people would do that to a child?"

Cullen opened his mouth, but words failed him. He didn't know what to say because he didn't understand it either.

"How could I," her breath hitched, "live so close

and not know what was happening?"

He couldn't stand seeing the pain in her eyes, and put his hand on Ruby's shoulder, giving it a light squeeze. She flinched and he pulled his hand back like it had touched a hot coal.

"I'm sorry," he said, taking a step back. "I wasn't going to hurt you."

The night air was cold and still. Cullen watched wisps of air come out of Ruby's mouth as she struggled to get control of her breathing. The nearly full moon was just creeping over the barn. In any other situation, him being out here alone with a pretty woman might be considered romantic. But as he watched that pretty woman break down in front of him, he knew exactly why he'd been led here. To fix what was broken.

Cullen took a tentative step toward her. Her eyes met his and in them he saw embarrassment and shame. Her shoulders slumped and she lowered her head. He slowly lifted his hand until his fingers touched her chin. He gently lifted it up until their eyes met.

"Ruby, I don't know what Cyrus did to you, but I'm guessing it wasn't good."

Ruby blinked as fresh tears poured out of her eyes. He could almost feel her pain. She tried to turn away, but he gently guided her head back until she was looking at him again.

"I'm not going to hurt you, Ruby," he said. "I've done a lot of things in my life that I'm not proud of, but I've never laid hands on a woman, or a child. Not all men are like Cyrus."

Her face crumpled and she started to cry. He pulled her into his arms, careful to keep the lantern a safe distance from her coat, and held her close. She buried her head in his shoulder and sobbed. He tried not to notice the way she fit perfectly in his arms, or the soft floral scent of her hair, but he couldn't help himself. *Stay*. The word ran through his mind again, followed by an image of the sawmill. This time he didn't push it aside.

Chapter Nine

Pastor Collins didn't show up mid-week, like he said he would. Even a week later, every time Ruby heard a strange noise outside, she'd pull open the door and peer down the road, expecting to see his buggy. She'd allowed her egg basket to nearly overfill, but she'd avoided taking them to town for fear of running into him. She wasn't sure what delayed his visit, but she knew it was only a matter of time before he came calling. Only a matter of time before Cullen would be on his way. Oh, Ruby knew he would leave eventually, but somewhere in the deepest, most private part of her soul, she hoped he would stay.

Cullen had kept himself busy working outside and in the barn. He'd been back and forth from Henzel's several times. Ruby suspected he'd been using the sawmill to cut some of the boards he repaired the paddock fence with, as well as the hole she'd blown in the side of the barn the day he'd arrived. She'd thanked God several times since then for her poor aim. There was an easiness about Cullen that Ruby admired. It was like he accepted the day, no matter what fell in his path. They hadn't talked about that night she'd broken down, but she felt like things between them had changed, if only just a little. She felt more comfortable around him.

Everett was starting to open up more too. After supper was cleaned up, Ruby would read him stories from the Bible. Cullen usually stayed to listen too, and seemed to enjoy hearing them. Everett particularly liked the story about Noah and the animals. He'd also started following Cullen around when he came home from school. Cullen didn't seem to mind, but Ruby wondered if it was a good idea to let the child become too attached to him. She was mulling that over when she heard the distinct sound of an approaching buggy. Her fingers went numb and her heart pounded in her chest. She closed her eyes, took a deep breath, and pulled the door open.

When she opened her eyes, Ruby was surprised to see that it wasn't Pastor Collins's buggy after all. She squinted her eyes and released a breath she hadn't even been aware she was holding. It was Lotty Gruby, Isaac and Eliza's mother. She couldn't imagine why Mrs. Gruby would come to see her. Her stomach clenched. *What if something had happened to Everett?*

Cullen came out of the barn and also looked to see who was coming. He strode toward the house and stood next to Ruby. She wasn't sure if he was being protective or curious, but either way, she didn't mind.

"You expecting company?" he asked.

"No, that's Isaac and Eliza's ma, I don't know why she's here," she glanced up at him, trying to gauge his expression. "You don't think something happened to Everett, do you?"

Their eyes met for a moment before he turned back to the approaching buggy. "I don't think so, she doesn't look upset."

Ruby looked at Mrs. Gruby more closely. Now that she was nearer, Ruby saw that Cullen was right. The woman was smiling, and she gave a little wave as she brought the buggy to a stop in front of the small house. Cullen went to give her a hand climbing down.

"Thank you," Mrs. Gruby said, smiling broadly at Cullen. "Would you mind reaching behind the seat and handing me that basket?"

Cullen did as she asked and turned his attention to Ruby. "I'll be getting back to work now, enjoy your visit," he smiled warmly, holding her gaze for a bit longer than necessary before he turned and walked toward the barn. Ruby watched him until he disappeared inside, then turned to Mrs. Gruby. Her face grew hot as she realized she hadn't even greeted the woman yet. She ran a hand across her hair, smoothing it back in place.

"I'm sorry," she said, giving Mrs. Gruby a hesitant smile. "Would you like to come in? I can put a fresh pot of coffee on."

Mrs. Gruby raised her eyebrows and grinned. "I'd like that very much."

Ruby held the door open and let her in. Aside from when Altar brought the quilt when she'd first arrived in Last Chance, she couldn't remember ever having a visitor at the farm. Cyrus didn't want people in the house, and Ruby didn't really have any friends. Did she? She thought about her visit with Faith and Altar. Were they friends? Could Lotty Gruby be a friend? The concept was as foreign to her as true love. It was something she'd read about, but never really experienced.

She put a fresh pot of coffee on the stove and sat at the table across from Mrs. Gruby. She looked to be only a few years older than Ruby, and nearly the same height, although Mrs. Gruby was considerably thicker around the middle. She had hair so dark it was nearly black, and bright blue eyes that twinkled in the light from the lantern. They sat in silence for a moment, and Ruby shifted uncomfortably in her chair. She didn't know what to say, and could feel her cheeks turning red.

"I meant to come sooner," Mrs. Gruby finally said.

Ruby's gaze shifted and it looked as though Mrs. Gruby was trying to decide if she should continue or not. "You did?"

The woman across from her nodded. "We'd heard about Mr. Fulton's...well, demise, and I wanted to offer my condolences," she paused and a pained expression crossed her face, "but I just couldn't bring myself to do it."

Ruby's eyes widened in surprise and she wasn't sure how to interpret what she'd just heard.

"Ruby...may I call you Ruby?

Ruby nodded. "Yes, of course."

Mrs. Gruby smiled. "Good. I'm Lotty, but you probably already knew that. I wanted to come, be a proper neighbor, but I just couldn't offer sympathy when I had none."

Ruby felt her jaw go slack.

"I'm sorry if I shocked you," Lotty continued. "Amos always tells me I'm too blunt, but I say life is too short to beat around the bush. What I really should be saying is that I'm sorry you were married to that man."

Ruby blinked, but remained silent. She'd never met anyone before that spoke as freely as Lotty.

"I can't tell how many times I wanted to come and visit, to get to know you. A woman can't have too many friends, you know? I'd seen you in church, and you looked like you could use one or two, if you don't mind my saying so."

The coffee was done and Ruby stood and poured them each a cup. Lotty took a bundle out of the basket she'd brought and unwrapped it. It looked to be a small bread-like cake. Ruby pulled two plates and forks out of the cabinet, along with a knife.

"I brought some of my famous gingerbread," Lotty grinned proudly. "Got me a blue ribbon at the fair with it."

Ruby had never heard of gingerbread, but the spicy, molasses-like smell was enticing. She wasn't sure what to do with it, so she handed Lotty the knife and allowed her to cut it and put it on the plates. Lotty took a sip of coffee and groaned.

"Why Ruby Fulton, this is the best cup of coffee I've had. What do you do to it?"

Ruby blushed. "I put eggshells in with the grounds."

Lotty's eyebrows shot up. "Whatever made you think to do that?"

Ruby shrugged. When she was at the orphanage, she often worked in the kitchen. One of the cooks showed her the trick, but she was reluctant to share that part of her past. "I just picked it up somewhere," she said vaguely.

Lotty looked at her for a moment, then nodded. "Well, before I leave, you must show me how you do that."

Ruby blushed, no one had ever asked her to show them anything. She sat a little straighter in the chair and took a tentative bite of the gingerbread. She closed her eyes and nearly groaned, it was so good. The cake was moist, not dry like most cakes were, and had a delicate balance of spices, along with a warm sweetness. She tasted cinnamon, but couldn't recognize the other flavors.

"You like it?"

Ruby opened her eyes, and nodded. "I've never tasted anything like it," she took another forkful and before she knew it, her plate was empty.

"Have another piece," Lotty said, pushing the gingerbread toward her.

Ruby gazed longingly at it, but shook her head. "I shouldn't."

Lotty chuckled. "You should. But if you won't have it now, I'll leave it here. Then you can have some later."

Ruby raised her eyebrows. "Thank you, that's very generous."

"Pish posh," she waved her hand in the air. "I should have brought you some a long time ago. Perhaps you can share some with your hired man," she raised her eyebrows. "He's quite handsome."

Ruby's face and ears turned hot, and she shifted her gaze to her empty plate. It was true, Cullen was a very handsome man. She tried her best to remember he was only there because she hired him. A man like that would never be interested in the likes of her.

"Does Pastor Collins know he's staying here?"

Ruby shook her head, then shrugged. "I'm not

sure, actually," she finally said. "Mrs. Purcell was talking to Mrs. Talley about it in the mercantile and he was there. I don't know if he heard them or not. He...he told me to expect him a few days ago, but he didn't come." The words poured out of her mouth in a rush.

Lotty pressed her lips together. "That man has nothing better to do than put his nose where it doesn't belong. If he wasn't a man of the cloth, I'd be tempted to give him a piece of my mind."

"I...I was there when he went to see Altar. After the twins were born." Ruby wasn't sure why she was telling Lotty this, but it felt so good to have someone to talk to about it. "He told her that having Wolfe there was sinful. He was going to make him leave, but Wolfe married her instead." Ruby chewed her lip for a moment. "He'll make Cullen leave," she said quietly.

Lotty reached across the table and put her hand on Ruby's. "Maybe Cullen will stay."

Ruby looked at the other woman for a moment,

then shook her head. She had nothing to offer a man like Cullen.

"God works in mysterious ways, Ruby Fulton," Lotty said. They were silent for a moment, then Lotty pulled her hand away. "Isaac and Eliza say that little Everett is doing well."

Ruby smiled and let out a sigh, grateful for the change of subject. "Yes, he seems to be doing better."

"That poor child, what he's been through," she made a tsking sound and pressed her lips together. "Shame that fine house is sitting empty and the sawmill is quiet. Amos had to go all the way to Grand Platte to get some boards last month. I told him to wait, but you know how men are when they have a mind to get something done."

"Lotty, do you know when Everett was born, by chance?"

Lotty frowned. "I'm not sure, I think it was sometime in the summer, but you know, the Henzel's were a quiet sort. If Gideon hadn't been running that sawmill, I don't know that anyone would have known them at all. Why do you ask?"

"He asked me when his birthday was," Ruby said. "But I don't know either."

Lotty shook her head in disgust. "How there could be people like that in the world, let alone in Last Chance, is beyond me. That little boy is lucky you took him in."

That was the second time this week she'd heard that, and for the second time that week she answered, "I think I'm the lucky one." She suddenly remembered Everett's wish about having a puppy of his own. "Lotty, do you know where I might find a puppy?"

The woman grinned. "As a matter of fact, I do."

They visited for a few more minutes, then Lotty stood and pulled on her coat. "I'm so glad I decided to come visit today. You are just a delight," she smiled warmly. "I'll be in touch about that puppy."

Ruby smiled and felt an unfamiliar lightness

spread through her. "Thank you, Lotty. I'm glad you came to visit too. Please come again, soon."

She walked Lotty out to her buggy and waved as she drove away. Once back inside, she pulled out the piece of parchment and stub of a pencil. She pictured Omega and Alpha's sweet little faces and the tender way Altar looked at them, and began to draw.

Chapter Ten

♥

Cullen watched Lotty Gruby drive away and smiled to himself. He wasn't sure how many friends Ruby had, but Mrs. Gruby was the first visitor she'd had since he'd been there. It made him wonder if that was something else Cyrus controlled. Cullen couldn't remember ever having such a dislike for someone he'd never met. Ruby hadn't said much about him, but it was pretty obvious to him that Cyrus had abused her. It made him angry just thinking about it.

He slipped back into the barn and finished mucking out the stalls. Cullen didn't mind the work, in fact, he enjoyed it. He found there was a certain peace that came at the end of an honest day's work. His attention kept wandering to the woman in the house, and he wondered what she was doing. She seemed to be on his mind an awful lot lately, and he found himself noticing little things about her. Like the way she'd smile when he told her he liked her cooking, or the way she'd look at Everett when he was telling her about his day at school, or the way she'd blush when she'd catch him looking at her. He'd never been affected by a woman this way before and wasn't sure what to make of it.

His rumbling stomach told Cullen it was past dinner time. He was surprised Ruby hadn't called him to the house yet, and began to wonder if her visit with Mrs. Gruby hadn't been a pleasant one after all. He walked up to the house and tentatively knocked on the door. A few seconds later, it opened and she stood looking back at him in surprise.

"Are you all right?" he asked.

She furrowed her brow. "Yes of course, why..." Her eyes grew wide. "Oh no, I lost all track of time. It's past dinner, isn't it?" She wiped her hands on her skirt. "I'll get something ready, it will just take me a minute."

Cullen held his hands up in a calming gesture. "It's all right, Ruby. I just wanted to make sure you were all right and that Mrs. Gruby's visit hadn't upset you." Something on the table behind her caught his eye, and he stepped inside to get a better look. It was a piece of paper and a tiny stub of a pencil. Ruby followed his gaze and a look of panic crossed her face.

"Cullen, wait," she placed a hand on his arm.

He reached the table and picked up the piece of parchment. It was a drawing of two infants laying side-by-side in a basket. It wasn't finished, but it had the same intricate details as the drawings he'd seen in the trunk. She had drawn all of them.

She snatched the paper out of his hands and slipped it into the cupboard. When she turned around, her cheeks were red and anger flashed in her eyes. "You weren't supposed to see that," she folded her arms across her chest and glared at him.

"It's a beautiful drawing," he said. "Why wouldn't you want me to see it? You're clearly very talented, you should be proud of it."

Ruby blinked rapidly and then shook her head. "I just didn't...it's not even done yet."

"There are two babies in this one. Do you know them?"

She narrowed her eyes at him. "What do you mean, this one?"

Cullen hesitated, but then continued. "The other drawings have only one child in them."

The color drained from Ruby's face except for the two red splotches on her cheeks. She took a step back and splayed her hand on her chest. "You...you were in my trunk? How could you?"

Cullen suddenly realized he had done something very wrong. At the time, it had seemed totally innocent. "I'm sorry. I didn't mean...I saw it and was curious, that's all."

"So you thought you'd open it? It wasn't yours. Those are my...my personal, private things."

"I don't know why you hide them," he tried to reason. "They're beautiful. The most beautiful drawings I've ever seen." Then realization struck. Cyrus. She'd hidden them from Cyrus. That also explained the various different sizes of paper. She drew on whatever she could find. His heart fell, and he felt ashamed. "I'm sorry, Ruby."

"Go," she said, as tears streamed down her face.

Cullen reached a hand out. "I didn't mean..." But she pulled away.

"Please, just go," she turned her back to him. He stood there for a moment and then did an about-face and walked out of the house.

Cullen retreated to the barn. He hadn't even felt this low when he'd been sentenced to prison. *What had he been thinking? How could he make this right?*

He had no idea. He had very little experience with women. He did know that the hurt he saw in her eyes, that he put there, was something he vowed never to put there again. She'd had enough hurt in her life, she didn't need him to cause more.

The sound of children's laughter interrupted his thoughts, and he stepped outside just in time to see Isaac and Eliza disappear over the hill, and Everett run toward the house. Cullen didn't know if Ruby was still upset, but he didn't want Everett to see her that way.

"Everett," he called, waving his hand. "Why don't you come here?" The little boy diverted his course and ran toward the barn.

"Hi, Mr. Parker," the boy grinned.

"I could use your help on something I'm making in the barn today, would you like that?"

The boy's eyes grew wide. "Yes, Mr. Parker, just let me go say hi to Miss Ruby and I'll be right back," he turned and started to run toward the house, but

Cullen caught his arm and pulled him to a stop.

"Why don't you wait a bit?" he said. "I think Miss Ruby might like to be alone for a little while."

Everett glanced from Cullen to the house and back. "Did you do something wrong?"

Cullen felt heat rise up his neck and into his face. He put his arm around the boy's shoulder and they walked into the barn. "Yes, I did."

Everett looked up at him. "Did you say you're sorry?"

"I did," he nodded.

The boy looked at him solemnly for a moment, then shrugged. "Miss Ruby is really nice; she won't be mad very long."

Cullen smiled at the boy's insight and prayed he was right.

A short time later, Ruby stepped into the barn. The rims of her eyes were still a little pink, but the anger was gone from them.

"Everett," she said. "Isaac and Eliza's Ma came to

visit today, and she brought some cake. I cut a piece and put it on a plate for you inside if you want it."

Everett's eyes grew big as saucers. "Cake? For me?" He ran to Ruby and wrapped his arms around her skirt. "Thank you, Miss Ruby," he said and ran out of the barn.

They stared at each other for a long moment, then she pointed at the project he'd been working on. "What's that?"

"I'm building a stanchion for the cow," he said. "Everett was helping me."

She tipped her head to the side and looked at it again.

"It holds the cow in place to make milking easier," he explained.

She nodded, and pulled her bottom lip in between her teeth, and drew in a deep breath.

Cullen's stomach tightened. *She was going to ask him to leave.* He tightened his grip on the hammer in his hand and held his breath, waiting for her to speak the words he didn't want to hear.

"Cullen, I...I'm sorry," she said.

Wait, what? Had he heard her right? "You're sorry?" He set the hammer down and took a step toward her. "You have nothing to be sorry about. I'm the one at fault here."

She held a hand up. "Let me finish."

He closed his mouth and nodded. He noticed something different about her, but he couldn't figure out what it was. She had the same brown dress and scuffed black shoes on that she always wore. Her hair was pulled back in the same tight knot. He watched her intently as she spoke.

"I shouldn't have gotten so upset with you this afternoon," she clasped her hands in front of her, but they were loose, not tight as they usually were. She lifted her chin slightly and continued. "I know you didn't mean any harm. Those drawings, those were...are the only things I have that are mine. Cyrus took everything else away, in ways you wouldn't understand. They are very personal to me. That's why I got so upset with you. I understand you were just trying to pay me a...a compliment."

All at once, Cullen realized what was different about her. She was standing straight and tall, as tall as a woman her size could stand, and she held his eyes the entire time she spoke. There was a strength and confidence about her that she'd never shown before. The odd tug Cullen had felt on his heart before suddenly felt more like a yank. His mind went blank. He opened his mouth, but it was like he'd forgotten what words were, and he merely nodded.

"All right then," she gave him a small smile and his stomach flipped. "I'm going back to make sure Everett doesn't eat the rest of the cake," she continued. "You're welcome to come have a piece too, if you'd like."

Cullen watched her leave and stared at the door for a few moments, while her words ran through his mind again. He squeezed his eyes shut when he thought about how foolish he must have looked just standing there, and mentally cursed himself. Even his brother, Ben, would have come up with something to say. He sat on the sawhorse and let his shoulders slump.

He didn't understand why he was feeling this way. He had a plan. Once the weather warmed up, he'd ride north. Some of the men he'd panned with in Deadwood were going to Lead, and Cullen knew he'd have no trouble getting hired at the Homestake Mine there. It was what he wanted to do. Wasn't it? He glanced at the tools and pieces of wood laying at his feet, and thought of the sawmill again. *Stay.*

He rose to his feet and looked out the door at the house. A thin ribbon of smoke rose from the chimney flue and Cullen thought about the little boy inside eating his cake while Ruby watched him. He remembered something his mother had told him when he was little and they were moving around. *Home is where you make it.* And he knew. He'd found his home.

The sound of an approaching horse and buggy interrupted his thoughts, and Cullen turned to see who was coming. A man in a black suit and black hat sat alone in the buggy. An uneasy feeling spread through him and he raced toward the house. He reached the door just as Ruby opened it.

"Pastor Collins," she gasped.

Chapter Eleven

♥

Ruby wrung her hands as Pastor Collins climbed out of his buggy. Cullen stood by her side and while she was glad he was there, she knew his presence would only serve to fuel the preacher's accusations. Everett came out of the house and stood next to her, holding onto her skirt.

"Who's that, Miss Ruby?" he whispered.

Before she could answer him, the preacher made his way around his horse and stood in front of them, his thin lips curled into a sneer. He was wearing the same black frock that he had on when Ruby had nearly run into him at the mercantile. His black, flat brim hat was pulled down low over brown hair that looked like it could use washing, and for some reason, Cyrus popped into Ruby's mind. Cyrus's hair was always in need of a wash too, as well as the rest of him. It had taken her weeks of cleaning and scouring before she could no longer smell him in the cabin. Even the smell of the chickens as they sheltered inside during the blizzards was preferable. She wondered if the preacher smelled as bad as Cyrus had too, and the thought sent a very inappropriate giggle up her throat. She slapped her hand over her mouth and coughed it away.

Barnaby Collins narrowed his eyes and glanced back and forth between her and Cullen. "Sinners!" he bellowed. Everett let out a strangled cry and ran into the house.

Cullen held his hand up. "Now wait just a minute," he said, and Ruby cringed.

Pastor Collins pointed his finger at Cullen, and puffed his chest out. He did that in church too, right before he began to moralize about the innate sinfulness of his congregation. Ruby wished she would have warned Cullen about Pastor Collins, but she'd been afraid to.

"The devil has a stronghold on this house. Thanks be to the Almighty God that I have been made aware of this transgression and am here to stamp out the sin that has gathered in this place." His gaze shifted and he stared into Ruby's eyes. "Mrs. Fulton, why have you taken to a life of sin since your husband's death? Living the life of a loose woman, and jeopardizing your eternal soul. This man, Cullen Parker, is nothing more than a drifter. You are choosing to lose your place in the Kingdom of the Almighty God for *him*?"

Cullen took a step forward and stood nearly toe to toe with the preacher. "She is not a loose woman," he growled. "I don't care if you're a man of the cloth or not, this woman has done nothing improper."

"So say you! The tongue of the devil cannot be

trusted. Would you condemn her soul in the name of lust? Brand her a harlot?"

Ruby's insides began to quiver and she wrapped her arms around her stomach. *What had she done? Nothing.* The word filled her mind as surely as if it had been shouted in her ear. *She had done nothing improper with Cullen Parker.* She lifted her head and straightened her shoulders.

"Pastor Collins, let me explain. It's not what you think."

He shook his head. "Are you married to this man?"

Ruby blinked. "N-n-no."

"Has Mr. Parker lived at this place, alone, with you, for weeks?"

Ruby's face grew hot and her cheeks flushed bright red. "Well, yes, but..."

The preacher lifted his hand. "Have you had a chaperone here with you?"

Ruby lowered her gaze. "No."

"I don't appreciate what you're trying to imply here, Pastor," Cullen broke in. "Mrs. Fulton is a fine, Godly woman. And while I may have been staying here, I have been sleeping in the barn. Alone. Not in the house. I wouldn't take advantage of her in that way."

"The devil speaks with a forked tongue. The damage has been done. The Good Book says, '*That whosoever looketh on a woman to lust after her hath committed adultery with her already in his heart*'. There is but one way to rectify this situation."

Ruby closed her eyes and waited for words she knew were coming.

"You must marry this woman."

Ruby's eyes flew open and it felt as though her entire body had gone numb. "What? No!"

"I'll do it," Cullen said.

Ruby's gaze snapped to Cullen's. *What was he doing?*

Pastor Collins clasped his hands in front of him.

"Very well…"

"No, wait! Cullen, you can't do this," Ruby hissed.

"He can, or you will both leave Last Chance," the preacher looked down his thin nose at her, almost as if daring her to defy him.

He'd make her leave? Where would she go? What about Everett? Fear gripped her like hands around her throat and she struggled to catch her breath. *Could he really do that?* She recalled what she'd heard at Altar's house the day Altar married Wolfe. She didn't know if he could, but she knew he would.

Cullen turned to the preacher. "Let me have a moment with her."

Pastor Collins raised one brow, then shrugged. "Very well."

Cullen grabbed her arm and pulled her toward the barn. They stopped in front of the door, still visible to the preacher, but out of earshot.

"Let me marry you, Ruby."

Ruby shook her head and closed her eyes. *This couldn't be happening. Her selfishness was going to cost him his dreams.* "I can't let you do that, Cullen." She lifted her eyes, silently pleading with him to be reasonable. "What about the gold mine in Dakota Territory? You said you could get a job there. You don't want to stay in this cursed town with a woman you don't love." A tear escaped her eye and trailed down her cheek.

Cullen lifted his hand and gently wiped it away. "I've been thinking," he said. "The town needs the sawmill. I have some gold, enough to buy the mill, I think."

Ruby shook her head, and Cullen placed his hands on her arms and looked deep into her eyes. A strange flutter coursed through her and she swallowed hard. His hands felt large on her shoulders, but in them she felt safety, not fear. He was not like Cyrus, of that she was sure. But could she trust him?

"Let me marry you, Ruby," he said in a low, gentle

tone. "You and Everett can have a proper home, and I can run the mill. It can be a marriage in name only, if you want."

Her eyes widened. "Why...why would you do that?"

"I was drawn to this town for a reason, Ruby. I don't know how to explain it. But I want to stay. If there's a day that you want to have more, then you will have to come to me. Until that day comes, I will be happy as we are. Marry me, Ruby."

She stared at him for a long moment. She didn't really have any other options, but it was more than that. There was something in his eyes that she'd never seen with Cyrus. She closed her eyes and drew in a shaky breath. "I will."

"I will never make you regret it," Cullen grinned. He took her hand and they walked to where the preacher impatiently waited.

"Have you seen the error of your sinful ways, Mrs. Fulton?"

Ruby opened to her mouth to speak, but Cullen squeezed her hand and she closed it.

"She has committed no sin, Pastor," he reiterated, and the preacher's mouth pressed into a thin line. "But she has agreed to marry me."

Pastor Collins's condescending demeanor disappeared and a wide grin spread across his face. "Praise the Holy God of the World that your souls will be saved."

Ruby felt as though she were watching herself in a dream. She could hear the preacher and Cullen talking, but the words passed through her ears and trailed off in the breeze. The next thing she knew, Pastor Collins was climbing back into his buggy and driving up the hill and away from her house. She glanced up at Cullen. *Had he really agreed to marry her? Why was the preacher leaving?* Her throat tightened and she couldn't catch her breath.

Cullen led her into the house and pulled a chair out for her to sit in. He poured a cup of coffee and handed it to her. She sipped the warm liquid greedily and felt herself relaxing, her breathing slowly returned to normal.

"Are you all right?" Cullen's concerned eyes gazed into hers.

She nodded. "I'm sorry, I don't know what happened," her cheeks flushed. "He left?"

Cullen nodded. "There needs to be witnesses. We will get married at church on Sunday."

Ruby stood in the doorway of the house and watched as Lotty brought her buggy to stop in front of the house for the second time that week. She couldn't imagine what would bring the woman by again so soon, but she didn't mind the intrusion. She'd been trying to wrap her head around the fact that in just a matter of days, she'd be a married woman again. It would be nice to be able to talk about it with someone. Lotty waved and climbed down. She reached behind the seat and pulled out a basket and a paper wrapped bundle.

"Hi Ruby, I'm guessing you didn't think you'd see me again so soon," she chuckled and followed Ruby into the house. She placed the basket and bundle on the table, and glanced at the cook stove. "Oh good, you have coffee on. We forgot to have you show me how you do that trick with the eggshells. I can't hardly drink my coffee at home now that I've had yours."

Ruby felt her face flush and she demonstrated to Lotty how she put clean, crushed eggshells in with the grounds before the coffee percolated.

"Well, I never," Lotty exclaimed. "That's a clever use for the shells."

Ruby poured two cups, and Lotty opened the basket and pulled out another gingerbread cake.

Once the cake was cut and on plates, Lotty clapped her hands.

"I heard in town that you are getting married! I just love a good wedding," she smiled, then frowned. "I also heard that Pastor Collins forced his hand on the matter."

Ruby nodded. "Yes, Cullen convinced me to say yes, but...," she paused. She didn't really know her new friend very well. Was this something friends would talk about?

Lotty placed her hand on Ruby's. "What is it, Ruby?"

Lotty looked so sincere that Ruby found herself spilling out everything. She told her how she'd prayed for Cyrus not to return, and how she hadn't wanted to take one of the letters that came from the advertisement that the town placed for grooms. How she'd feared Cullen would leave, but never considered he'd marry her and offer a marriage in name only. When she was done, Lotty just sat quietly for a moment.

Ruby's stomach rolled. *Had she said too much?*

"I can't blame you one bit for not wanting to take one of those letters after what you went through with Cyrus," Lotty said, taking a bite of cake. "And I think you'd be surprised to find you weren't alone in wishing he wouldn't come back."

Ruby stopped chewing her cake and stared at Lotty for a moment.

"It's true, he was a vile man. I'd say more, but being a Christian woman, I can't." She dismissed the conversation with a wave of her fork. "Enough about him. I want to talk about your wedding."

Ruby blushed and tried to hide her face behind her cup of coffee.

"I had a feeling about that man," Lotty's eyes sparkled with amusement. "Where is he? I didn't see him when I got here."

"He went to Grand Platte to do some business. He wants to buy the sawmill."

Lotty raised her eyebrows. "That is wonderful

news! Amos will be happy to hear that, as well as half the town I'm sure. When is the wedding?"

"Sunday, at the church," Ruby murmured. The idea of getting married in front of the entire town had her nerves pulled so tight, she could hardly function. Getting married to Cullen was one thing, but to do it in front of so many people....

"Oh my, that's just a couple days away. Hope you don't mind," she reached for the paper-wrapped bundle and handed it to Ruby. "But I took it upon myself to bring you a dress to wear," she glanced at Ruby's worn brown dress and hesitated.

Ruby watched her gaze shift and felt heat rise up her neck. She only had two dresses, and both were of the same plain brown, now threadbare fabric. She'd been eyeing some fabric at the mercantile, but couldn't bring herself to spend the money on something for herself. Not when she had a growing boy to feed and clothe.

"I wasn't sure if you had something special to

wear," Lotty said carefully, "and every woman should have something special to wear at their wedding."

Ruby slowly unwrapped the package, trying to blink back the tears that burned in the back of her eyes. She let out a soft gasp as she lifted out a beautiful calico dress. The fabric was covered with delicate blue flowers, and Ruby ran her fingers along the shell buttons that went up the front of it.

"Oh Lotty," she breathed. "It's beautiful," she gazed longingly at the dress, then shook her head and slid it across the table. "I can't possibly accept such a fine gift."

Lotty slid it back. "Nonsense. Besides, it's not new, but it is clean," she eyed Ruby up and down. "Of course, we'll have to take it in some."

Ruby held the dress to her chest while tears streamed down her face. She'd never had anything so beautiful to call her own before. "Thank you, Lotty."

Lotty wiped her eyes. "Now stop that nonsense, and put it on before that man of yours gets home. We need to make it fit."

Chapter Twelve

♥

Cullen rode back into Last Chance a happy man. He'd gotten a premium price for his gold at the assayer's office in Grand Platte, and was hoping his luck would carry forward when he met with Judge Bringegar. He guided Ghost up Stagecoach Road and looked at the businesses and people he passed with different eyes than he had a month ago when he'd first ridden into town. This was now his home. A lightness filled him at the thought, spreading a warmth through him that couldn't be permeated even by the cold northwest wind.

He tethered his mare to the post in front of

a building next to the Sheriff's Office with a sign that read Judge J. Bringegar on it. He gave Ghost an affectionate pat on the neck before walking up to the door and stepping inside. A heavy-set man with white hair and a white beard sat behind a large wooden desk, and greeted Cullen when he came in. The judge had an authoritative look about him, and Cullen was suddenly reminded of the judge that had sentenced him to San Quentin. His stomach rolled and his mouth suddenly went dry. *He wasn't the same person anymore. He'd changed.*

Cullen removed his hat and cleared his throat. "I'm looking for Judge Bringegar."

The man leaned back in his chair and made a steeple out of his fingers. "That would be me, what can I help you with?"

"I'd like to inquire about purchasing the Henzel's property, including the sawmill."

Judge Bringegar's eyebrows shot up. "And who might you be?"

Cullen extended his hand, "Cullen Parker, sir."

"You're not from Last Chance, are you?"

"No, sir, but I intend to make it my home."

The judge narrowed his eyes. "Well, Mr. Parker, I'm sorry but Gideon and Ida Henzel had a son. As their sole survivor, the estate would pass down to him."

Cullen ran his fingers along the brim of his hat. "Everett."

"Excuse me?"

"Everett. That's the name of their son. I wanted to talk to you about him, too."

"How so?"

"I'd like to adopt him," Cullen smiled. *This was going to work out better than he thought.*

Judge Bringegar leaned forward and spread his hands on the top of desk. "That's a might bit convenient, isn't it?"

Heat rose up Cullen's neck and into his face. "No, sir, it's not like that at all."

He spent the next thirty minutes explaining the situation to the judge. The only part he left out was that his marriage to Ruby was to be in name only. He didn't figure that was anyone else's business.

They finally agreed that after his marriage to Ruby was final, Cullen and Ruby, as a married couple could adopt Everett. Cullen would then pay the agreed upon price for the property, and its contents, including the saw mill. That money would be put aside for Everett in a trust until he was of age. The amount was far less than Cullen expected to pay, and he walked out of the office with an extra swing in his step.

He climbed back in his saddle and continued through town, turning at the livery. He stopped at the mercantile and, after securing Ghost, stepped inside.

"Mr. Parker," the man behind the counter greeted him. "Good to see you again. I hear congratulations are in order?"

Cullen's brows furrowed for just a moment before he realized what the man was talking about. His face broke into a wide grin. "Yes, thank you."

Christmas was only days away, and Cullen wandered through the aisles, looking for something he could give Ruby as a gift. He'd already decided, once they were married, he would bring her here and let her pick out what she wanted for some new dresses and shoes. It was clear that Cyrus couldn't care less if his wife was dressed in rags. Cullen pushed the thought aside. *It didn't matter anymore. She was going to be his wife to care for now.*

He saw the stack of parchment paper and remembered the drawing of the twin infants she'd been working on. Seeing no other paper, Cullen took two new graphite pencils and went to the counter.

"Do you have a sketch book, by chance?" he asked. "I didn't see anything that looked like one, but I don't know that I've ever seen one."

The man brought his hand up and twisted the

end of his long mustache. "No," he finally said, "I don't believe we've had one of them in for quite some time."

Cullen's shoulders sagged. *He'd have to find something else.* He was just about to turn to look through the aisles again when the man snapped his fingers.

"Wait just a minute, let me run to the back and look. I might have something."

Cullen watched him disappear through a swinging door and said a quick prayer that he'd find one. He frowned while he tried to remember what the man's name was. While he was waiting, the door to the mercantile opened and a pretty woman with light brown hair walked in. She placed a pile of mail on the counter and gave Cullen a curious glance.

The swinging doors parted and the man stepped through them, a triumphant smile on his face. His glance slid to the woman.

"Thank you, Mrs. Thornton."

"Do you have anything to go out, Mr. Talley?" she asked.

Mr. Talley. That was it!

"Not today," Mr. Talley gestured to Cullen. "Have you met Mr. Parker?"

Her eyebrows raised and a warm smile crossed her face. "No, I haven't had the pleasure. You're marrying Ruby Fulton on Sunday, right?"

Their marriage seemed to be the talk of the town. Cullen returned her smile and nodded. "Nice to meet you, ma'am."

"Ruby is a fine woman," Mrs. Thornton said. "She deserves better than what she had." She cast him a pointed glance.

Cullen rubbed the back of his neck and nodded again. "Yes, ma'am."

Her mouth curved back into a smile, and she gave a little wave as she opened the door. "See you Sunday then."

Cullen watched her leave, then turned back to

Mr. Talley. He held up a leather bound sketch book. *It was perfect.*

"Is this what you had in mind?"

"Yes, I'll take it. Can you wrap it, along with these?" He handed Mr. Talley the pencils. "I'll also take a bag of gumdrops and a peppermint stick.

"Yes, of course," Mr. Talley replied and wrapped the sketch book in paper, tying it with a string. "That is a fine gift, if you don't mind me saying so."

"I hope she thinks so," Cullen smiled and gathered his purchases. He was anxious to get home to see Ruby and Everett. Even Ghost picked up her pace as the familiar barn came into view.

Cullen hid the sketchbook in the barn, along with the gift he'd been making for Everett, and made it into the house just in time for supper. He sat across from Ruby at the small table, while Everett perched on the side of the wood box, and closed his eyes while Ruby said Grace. He had so much to be thankful for.

While they ate, Cullen told them about his trip

to Grand Platte, and that he'd worked out a purchase deal for the Henzel's property. They'd be able to move there right after the wedding.

Everett went still and a crease appeared above his eyebrows. "Will I have to stay in my room all the time again when we go back?"

Cullen and Ruby exchanged glances, and Ruby brought her hand up and covered her mouth.

"No, Everett," Cullen said. "In fact, I was thinking that we could make a ladder and make you a new room in the loft. How would that be?"

A wide smile appeared on Everett's small face. "I can help you?"

"Of course you can."

Everett lifted his hands and clapped. In his excitement, he bumped his plate, which bumped his glass, spilling milk all over the table. Everett jumped off his seat and backed away from the table, his eyes filled with tears. Cullen watched in disbelief as the boy backed into the wall and sunk to his knees, putting his small arms protectively over his head.

"I'm sorry, I didn't mean it," he sobbed. "I'll be more careful."

Ruby had leaped out of her chair, and was frantically wiping the milk off the table, her face pale and pinched, and her eyes glassy with unshed tears. Cullen's gaze traveled back and forth between the two of them. He felt a sharp pain in his chest and a heaviness settled over him as he witnessed the damage the past had inflicted on the two people he cared about most.

He reached forward and stilled Ruby's frantic scrubbing. Their eyes met and, he could see apprehension etched in her face. Cullen gave a slight shake of his head and gestured toward the chair.

"It's all right, sit," he said gently, and rose to his feet. "It's just a little milk. We have more."

Ruby sat and stared as he walked over to where Everett sat hunched over in a little ball, and pulled the boy into his arms. Cullen said nothing, just held

the child close and let him cry. As his sobs subsided, Everett's muscles began to relax and his little
arms slipped around Cullen's neck. His heart swelled
and warmth spread through his limbs. He glanced at
Ruby, who held his gaze, her cheeks glowing and her
eyes bright, and he knew he'd found love. He only
hoped she would one day love him back.

Cullen stood at the front of the church in his
best clothes, and shifted uncomfortably under the
stares of what had to be the entire population of Last
Chance. Nearly every bench in the church was full,
and all eyes were on him. His heart pounded in his
chest and he drew in a deep breath to steady himself,
and tried to inconspicuously wipe his sweaty palms
on his pants.

When Pastor Collins insisted they marry at the church, Cullen thought they'd just have a quiet ceremony after the service on Sunday. But when Lotty Gruby showed up to collect Ruby hours before the service was scheduled to start, he knew that's not how it would play out.

The organist played a few notes to get everyone's attention and Pastor Collins moved to his spot just behind Cullen. As music filled the church, movement in the back attracted Cullen's attention. A beautiful woman in a pretty blue dress stepped into view and Cullen drew in a sharp breath when he realized it was Ruby.

Her brown hair, which she always wore pulled back in a tight knot, was loose and flowed down her back nearly to her waist. It softened her features somehow, and the flush in her cheeks made her face positively glow. Butterflies danced in his stomach as she hurried down the center aisle and came to a stop next to him, her uncertain gaze meeting his. He wanted to tell her how beautiful she looked, but when he opened his mouth nothing came out.

"We are gathered here today to join these two souls in the holy vows of matrimony," Pastor Collins proclaimed. Cullen stared at Ruby and tried to pay attention to the words coming out of the preacher's mouth. His only focus was on her, but somehow, he managed to hear enough to know when to say *I do*.

"You may now kiss the bride," Pastor Collins proclaimed, and Ruby dropped her gaze, her face blushing furiously. Cullen raised his hand and gently lifted her chin with one finger until she was once again looking into his eyes. Recalling his promise to her, he leaned forward and brushed the softest of kisses against her lips. It took every bit of self-control he had to pull away, and when he did, the look on her face gave him hope that maybe, just maybe she felt the same way he did.

Chapter Thirteen

♥

Ruby stared at the thin gold band on her finger and admired the way it shone in the light of the lantern as she turned her hand this way and that. Cyrus hadn't given her a ring and, to be honest, she hadn't minded. It made this one all the more special. She thought about their wedding. It was hard to believe just a day earlier, she'd been Ruby Fulton, widow. Now she was Mrs. Cullen Parker. She liked the way that sounded.

There were far more people at the church than she'd expected. She'd been grateful for Lotty's help getting ready and while she hadn't liked being the center of attention as she made her way down the aisle, she felt elated at the surprise and admiration she'd seen in Cullen's eyes. The blue calico dress made her feel almost pretty and she'd received so many compliments, she was filled with an unfamiliar sense of confidence. She found herself relishing in everyone's happiness and well wishes, and it was hard not to believe she'd welcomed a newfound hope of a life she never dreamed she could have.

Cullen had moved into the house from the barn when they'd come home. He'd reiterated that he would keep his promise and should anything change between the two of them, it would be up to her to make that happen, even going so far as to place a pillow between them so she might be more comfortable. She'd lain awake most of the night, listening to the quiet sounds of his deep breaths as he slept next to her, and wondered if a man like him could ever love a woman like her.

"Is it almost time?" Everett's voice pulled Ruby

out of her reflection. The child looked up at her with such hope and anticipation in his eyes that she could hardly bear to make him wait any longer to open his gifts.

"Soon. We need to wait for Cullen to finish chores."

"I hope he hurries," he glanced at the two small packages on the table. One for him, and the other for Cullen.

"Why don't you practice your letters while we wait?"

Everett's brow furrowed. "I don't think I can."

Ruby's gaze slid to the slate laying on his pallet. "Why not?"

"My fingers are too excited to make letters."

Ruby laughed and pulled him in for a quick hug. The door opened and Cullen stepped inside. Ruby could see snow swirling all around outside behind him, and gave a quick prayer of thanks for the blessing of shelter and warmth on this cold Christmas day.

Cullen had two large, paper wrapped bundles in his arms and he carefully placed them on the table next to the other two. The back of Ruby's throat tightened as she watched Everett practically burst with excitement. Cullen was good for the child. *He's good for you too.*

He shrugged out of his coat and hung it on the pegs, then took a seat at the table. Ruby poured him a cup of coffee and he gave her a grateful smile. She loved the way his eyes crinkled at the corner when he smiled. *It's a marriage in name only*, she reminded herself, and averted her attention to Everett, who by now had climbed onto the side of the wood box, his elbows propped on the table and head resting on his hands.

"If you stare at those packages any harder, Everett, your eyes are going to fall out of your head," Cullen chuckled. Ruby bit back a smile as Everett turned to Cullen, a sober expression on his face.

"Can that really happen?"

Cullen ruffled the boy's hair. "No, it can't really happen. It just means you're looking at something too hard."

Relief washed over Everett's face and he let out a little giggle. "That would be a little funny though, eyeballs rolling all over," he giggled again and slid a glance at Ruby. "Don't you think so, Miss Ruby?"

Ruby raised her eyebrows and tried not to smile. "I think that's enough talk about eyeballs."

Everett looked at Cullen and shrugged, a mischievous grin on his face. "Is it time now?" he asked.

Cullen glanced at Ruby and raised his eyebrows. While she didn't want to make the child wait any longer, she felt it was important to honor the true meaning behind Christmas. "I think we should read the story about when baby Jesus was born first. After all, that's what Christmas is really about."

Disappointment flashed across Everett's face, but was quickly replaced with anticipation as he ran to retrieve the Bible. He stopped in front of Cullen.

"Can Cullen read it this time?"

Ruby looked at Cullen and raised her eyebrows. Cullen nodded and Everett handed him the Bible. He walked past the wood box and stood next to her. "Can I sit with you and listen, Miss Ruby?"

She pulled him onto her lap and wrapped her arms around him, relishing in the warmth and comfort his little body provided as they listened to Cullen's deep baritone tell the story of how Jesus was born. Ruby couldn't remember a time in her life when she felt more at peace.

"And suddenly there was with the angel a multitude of the heavenly host praising God, and saying, Glory to God in the highest, and on earth peace, good will toward men," he finished and closed the book.

They sat in silence for several moments before Everett began squirming on Ruby's lap. She gave him one last squeeze before he slid off and returned to sit on his wood box. Cullen placed one of the packages he'd brought in with him in front of Everett and Ruby's eyes widened when he placed the other in front of her. She hadn't expected anything from him, and did her best to blink back the tears that threatened to spill over her eyelids as she picked up the packages she'd made. She placed one in front of Everett, and saw the same surprise in Cullen's eyes as she handed him the other.

Everett looked at Ruby, his pale brown eyes searching hers for permission. She nodded and he reached for the package she'd given him, then hesitated, his small fingers touching the twine she'd used to tie it together.

"What's wrong, Everett?"

"If I open it, it won't be there anymore," he said sadly.

Ruby felt a tug on her heart. "Yes, but if you don't open it, you won't know what's inside it."

Everett nodded and pulled the twine. Inside the package was a little blue shirt Ruby made him out of the fabric she'd purchased at the mercantile, and two gumdrops. He held the shirt tightly against his chest and closed his eyes for a moment.

"Thank you, Miss Ruby," he finally said. "May I have one of the candies?"

The back of Ruby's throat burned and her nose tingled as she nodded her head. Everett popped the candy into his mouth and reached for the package from Cullen. This time he didn't hesitate but unwrapped it right away, revealing a wooden ark.

Cullen reached across the table and slid a compartment open revealing a storage area inside the ark. Everett's mouth dropped open as he watched Cullen tip the ark on its side and a little wooden plank fell out, followed by several pairs of carved animals.

Ruby recognized pairs of sheep, cows, horses, several different kinds of birds, and pigs. Cullen gave the ark one last shake and two carved figures toppled onto the table.

"It's Noah!" Everett exclaimed, picking up one of the figures and examining it. "Noah and his animals!"

"It's incredible," Ruby breathed, reaching for one of the carved birds. She looked at Cullen. "You made this?"

A flush crept up his neck and he nodded.

"When...when did you have time? The craftsmanship is incredible."

"At night," he replied, with a slight shrug.

"It's really mine?" Everett looked at Cullen in disbelief.

Cullen nodded, and Everett looked back at his gift in wonder. "Thank you, Mr. Parker," he said, his voice filled with awe. His gaze shifted to Ruby. "Now your turn, Miss Ruby!"

Ruby felt her cheeks flush as she reached for the gift in front of her. It was the second time in a week she'd been given a gift she hadn't expected. She carefully untied the string and unfolded the paper, revealing a brown leather covered sketch book and two pencils. A soft gasp escaped her lips and she covered her mouth with her hands.

"Don't you like it, Miss Ruby?" Everett asked.

Ruby shook her head, then nodded. Tears clouded her vision as she tentatively reached out a hand and ran her finger along the smooth leather. "I love it, Everett," her eyes shifted to Cullen. "Thank you," was all she could manage.

"Then how come you're crying?"

"Sometimes people cry when they're happy too," Cullen answered.

"Oh," Everett glanced back and forth between Cullen and Ruby, then shrugged. "It's your turn now, Mr. Parker," he said gleefully, leaning forward on his elbows.

Cullen picked up the small package and unwrapped a shirt identical to Everett's. He ran his fingers along the fine stitches and knew it must have taken her hours to sew both shirts by hand.

"Oh!" Everett exclaimed. "It's just like mine, we can match!"

Cullen chuckled and looked at Ruby, who was still sitting in stunned silence. "Thank you, I've never had such a fine shirt."

"I made something," Everett said, sliding off the stool and rushing to his pallet. He dropped to his knees and fished under his blanket for a moment. He pulled out a folded piece of paper and handed it to Ruby with a triumphant grin. "Miss Ree—I mean Mrs. Taylor gave me the paper. We were supposed to draw what we wanted for Christmas."

Ruby unfolded the paper and brought a hand up to her mouth. She was unable to stop the tears that flowed down her cheeks as she looked at the drawing Everett had made. It was similar to the one she'd seen on his slate of the two figures representing him and her, with the house and the dog. Only in this drawing, the dog was slightly more recognizable as a dog and a third figure joined the other two and the house was somewhat larger.

"Mrs. Taylor said that was a family," he pointed

to the figures, then looked at Ruby, his expression suddenly serious. "Are we a family?"

"Yes, Everett," Cullen answered, and Ruby could hear a thickness in his voice that wasn't usually there. "We are a family."

"Then...does that mean you're my new pa? And Miss Ruby is my new ma?"

Cullen cleared his throat. "Would you like that, Everett?"

The boy's eyes filled with tears as he nodded his head and ran into Cullen's arms.

Chapter Fourteen

Cullen and Ruby drove the wagon into Last Chance a couple of days after Christmas. The first place they stopped was to see Heather Barnes, the town's midwife. Heather had indeed been present when Everett was born, and kept detailed records of all births she attended. After a few minutes of looking through her records, she smiled triumphantly.

"It's June third." Her smiled faded. "Poor Ida, had such a hard time. We almost lost her." Heather looked lost in thought for a moment, then looked back at Ruby. "It's so good that you've taken Everett in. He's a sweet boy."

"Thank you," Ruby said shyly. "I'm glad you had the records."

"You're welcome, and congratulations again. Your wedding was lovely."

Next, they met with Judge Bringegar to sign the papers, making Everett's adoption official. Cullen also signed the papers for the Henzel property, and told the Judge that for the time being, they were going to hold onto the Fulton place. Cullen knew that land prices would continue to increase and he hoped that by waiting, they'd be able to sell the small parcel for a larger profit at a later time.

They drove from there to the mercantile where, despite Ruby's protests, Cullen had her select several bolts of fabric so she could make herself some new dresses, as well as clothing for their growing son. It was still odd to think that in a matter of days, he'd gone from being a single man to being a husband and a father, but Cullen found it suited him just fine. He also had her select new pairs of shoes for both herself and Everett. Mrs. Talley was more than happy to help Ruby with her selections, and after adding a few dry goods, Cullen paid Mr. Talley and loaded the wagon with their purchases.

"Can we stop at Altar Penn—Laingsburg's home for a minute? I'd like to give this to her," she held up a roll of parchment. She'd finished the drawing of Altar's twins, and Cullen thought it was her best yet.

"Of course," he nodded, and she gave him directions. He helped her out of the wagon and told her he'd wait, but to take her time.

"I'll just be a minute," she smiled and hurried up the path to the front door. He watched as the door opened, and Wolfe let her inside giving a quick nod of his head in Cullen's direction before he closed the door behind her. True to her word, a few minutes later, the door opened again and she waved over her shoulder as she hurried back to the wagon.

"You didn't have to rush on my account," he said, wondering if he should have offered to go with her.

He'd met Altar, Wolfe, and the twins at their wedding and looked forward to getting to know them better, but he'd hoped to be able to pick up Everett at school before he left with the Gruby children. Today was moving day.

"It's fine, the twins were just getting ready to go down for a nap, and Altar looked like she could use one too," Ruby said as she settled next to him on the seat.

"Did she like her gift?"

Her face flushed, and she looked down at her hands, folded in her lap. "She did, very much."

Cullen knew it had taken a lot of courage for Ruby to give Altar something so personal, and he was proud of her. He clicked his tongue and with a snap of the reins, the wagon headed toward the school. Cullen sat proudly next to his wife and nodded a greeting to several people as they drove through the town. Everett was pleasantly surprised to see them waiting for him and he readily climbed into the back of the wagon. He told them in great detail about the game of kick the can they'd played at recess, and before long they were at their new home.

Cullen lifted Ruby out of the wagon and held her in his arms as he walked toward the house.

She tilted her head and arched a brow. "What are you doing, Cullen? Put me down."

"It's tradition for the groom to carry the bride into their new house," he said. "I didn't feel the cabin was truly ours, but this," he opened the door and stepped inside, "this is our house." He gingerly set her down, holding her a bit longer than necessary before reluctantly letting her go.

"Come with me, I want to show you something," he smiled, and took her by the hand. He led her to the small room behind the fireplace where Everett's bed had been.

"Cullen, I don't...," she began, then gasped as they entered the room. Against the wall stood a brand new Singer sewing machine. He'd had Mr. Talley special order it for him from Grand Platte, and had made arrangements for it to be delivered.

Ruby walked up to the machine and ran her fingers along the curve of the black machine and across the wood cabinet. She turned to him and shook her head. "How...when...it's too much, Cullen."

He put his finger on her lips to quiet her. "It's not," he said softly. "You deserve this, and more."

She pulled his hand down. "But the cost, surely we can't afford such an extravagance," she looked back over her shoulder and gestured toward the front of the house. "And all the purchases today..." she trailed off.

"I had more gold than I thought," he said simply. "And you let me worry about what is an extravagance and what isn't from now on," Cullen looked down at her wide brown eyes and his gaze trailed to her lips. *Let her come to you*. He cleared his throat and took a step back, then another, needing to put some distance between them before he broke his promise to her.

"Pa, can we put my ladder up?" Everett ran into the room and stopped short. "What's that?" he pointed to the machine.

"It's a sewing machine. It's so your Ma can make us clothes easier."

"It's very shiny," he examined the machine from a safe distance, then turned back to Cullen. "Can we get the ladder?"

After they were done opening their gifts on Christmas day, Everett insisted they start working on his ladder so it would be ready when they moved.

"Yes, let's get your ladder," he gave Ruby a wink before following Everett out of the house.

Spring was approaching and Cullen had been

busy getting the mill up and running again. He'd made several trips to Grand Platte to talk to the mill owner there, getting tips and ideas for improvements he wanted to make to his own mill once he could afford it. So far, there'd been a slow, but steady stream of customers, and Cullen was enjoying getting to know the people from town. Some of the men even brought their wives with them so they might visit a bit with Ruby while the men took care of business, and Lotty was a regular visitor.

He and Ruby had settled into an easy routine and although the pillow still rested between them at night, Cullen found he very much enjoyed being married to her. Her personality shone through more each day, as did Everett's. She'd sit in the rocking chair each night after supper and read story after story from the Bible, while Everett played with his ark.

After some trial and error, and some help from Lotty, Ruby had mastered the sewing machine, and had been busy making not only some new, much-needed clothing, but new curtains to hang in the windows. She loved the large cook stove that was in the house, and Cullen had gone on several successful hunting trips, bringing home rabbits, squirrels, and even a wild turkey. Ruby was a fine cook and had actually had to let out some of his pants.

Frequently, he'd catch her watching him when she didn't think he could see, and she often found silly reasons to come check on him while he was working in the mill. It gave him hope that someday soon, she'd come to him and tell him she loved him too.

It was late in the afternoon and Cullen was adjusting the belt on the saw, when a man on horseback came down their road. He straightened and wiped his hands on an old rag, then stepped out of the mill to get a closer look. He felt his stomach clench as he recognized the rider. It was his brother, Ben. *How had Ben found him, and what was he doing here?* Cullen squinted his eyes and looked farther down the road, but there was no sign of Frank.

Ben tipped his hat as he brought the tired-looking animal to a stop and climbed down from the saddle. He looked tired, and significantly older than the thirty-three years of age that Cullen knew him to be.

"What do you want, Ben?" Cullen asked, glancing at the house and saying a quick prayer that Ruby hadn't seen him ride in through the window.

"Frank's dead," he said somberly.

Cullen felt the air leave his lungs and he took a step back as if he'd been struck by an invisible force. "What happened?"

Before Ben could answer, Ruby stepped out of the house and waved. Ben glanced over and waved back. "You get married?" he looked at Cullen incredulously. "That your wife?"

Cullen felt his muscles tense. He hadn't planned to tell Ruby about his past. He'd been content to leave it where it was. Behind him. Now, it was standing right in front of him, waiting to be reckoned with.

"Hi Pa," he heard Everett call seconds before he saw the boy running toward the house.

"You're a pa, too?" Ben frowned and scratched the side of his head as if trying to figure out if it were possible for Cullen to have had a child since he'd last seen him.

Cullen glanced at Ruby, who was still standing in the doorway of the house, and his stomach tightened. *He should have told her before they got married.* He'd used the pardon he'd gotten from the governor of California to rationalize it in his mind. He figured if the state of California wiped his sins off their records, then he could too. Only, Ben knew his sins. And Ben couldn't keep secrets. After being married to someone like Cyrus, Cullen knew Ruby wouldn't take kindly to finding out she'd married a convict.

Ruby walked toward them, a friendly smile on her face and Cullen's mouth went dry. Ben removed his hat as she drew near, and she stopped next to

Cullen and looked up at him with her beautiful brown eyes, waiting for him to introduce her to the man that would take everything away from him.

"Cullen?" she furrowed her brow when he didn't say anything.

"Hi, ma'am," Ben smiled broadly at her. "I'm Ben Parker, Cullen's big brother."

Chapter Fifteen

♥

"What do you mean you spent four years in prison?" Ruby's head swam and she clutched her stomach. *Surely she misheard him.*

"I'm not the same person anymore," Cullen said, his eyes pleading with her to understand.

It had been a shock to find out Cullen had a brother, but Ruby couldn't have imagined that she'd find out she was married to a stagecoach robber. A thief. *She should have known he was too good to be true.*

Ruby rose to her feet and paced back and forth in their bedroom. After Ben had introduced himself, she invited him to join them for supper. She'd thought Cullen was acting a little strange, but attributed it to the surprise of his brother showing up unexpectedly. He was uncharacteristically quiet while she finished preparing the meal, and twice had tried to take her aside to talk to her. She should have known then that something was wrong. But, not wanting to be rude to their guest, had told Cullen they could talk later.

It hadn't taken her long to realize that something wasn't quite right with Ben. While he seemed very nice, there was a certain vacancy behind his eyes that she recognized in some the children she'd seen at the orphanage that the nuns referred to as simpleminded. She watched Ben and Everett play with the ark, and it was almost as if Everett was playing with another child. It was during the meal that she'd found out that Cullen had another brother who had been killed while trying to rob a train.

Ruby had quickly changed the subject and sent an objecting Everett to bed a little earlier than usual with an extra hug and kiss. She'd have to figure out how to undo the little bit that'd he'd heard later. Once Everett was up in his loft, Ruby sat at the table with Ben and Cullen and listened to Ben tell story after story about how they had robbed stagecoaches, and how Cullen was supposed to help them rob the train the previous fall but had disappeared in the night. Cullen seemed to shrink lower and lower in his chair. It was all Ruby could do not to throw them both out, but her compassion for the simple man, and the fact that there was still snow on the ground won out, and she reluctantly agreed to let him stay in the barn.

Now, she was regretting that decision. After Ben was settled in the barn, a very contrite Cullen came into the house and told her the rest. At least that's what he said. She didn't know how she could believe him. An image of the sewing machine filled her mind and Ruby's stomach dropped. She collapsed on the bed, letting her hands fall to her sides.

She looked up at Cullen through tear filled eyes.

"The gold..."

He paused, then turned pale and shook his head vehemently. "No," he dropped to his knees in front of her and held her hands. "The gold wasn't from a robbery. I panned that gold in Deadwood, Ruby. I swear."

She pulled her hands away and turned her head. "I think you better go out to the barn with your brother."

Cullen nodded and quietly left the house. Ruby sat back down on the bed and covered her face with her hands and cried. *Cyrus had been right. She was nothing but bad luck, and bad luck attracted bad luck.*

The next day Ruby had Cullen hitch Buckshot up to the buggy. She needed to get away. To think. To talk to her friend. They hadn't spoken except what was necessary as to not upset Everett. She brought the buggy to a stop in front of the Gruby house. Lotty opened the door and took one look at Ruby's red, swollen eyes and sent Amos out to the barn to find something to do. Ruby climbed down and Lotty put an arm around her and led her into the house.

"Ruby, what happened?"

Ruby wiped her eyes and told Lotty everything. The woman sat across from her in total silence. It was the first time that Ruby had seen her speechless.

"I don't know what to do," Ruby's shoulders slumped.

"That's quite a story," Lotty said.

"He says he's changed."

"Do you believe him?"

"I don't know." Ruby thought of all the times she'd been told at the orphanage that she was going to finally be adopted, only to find out that another, prettier girl was chosen instead. And all the times

Cyrus told her he'd taken care of something, only for her to find out that he hadn't. "I'm not sure I can," she admitted.

"Has he given you a reason not to?"

Ruby thought about that for a minute. "No," she admitted.

Lotty let out sigh. "He was on his way to Dakota Territory when he came to Last Chance, right?"

Ruby nodded.

"He had money. He didn't *need* to answer your advertisement."

Ruby lifted her eyes and listened.

"Now, admittedly," she said holding Ruby's gaze, "I don't know Cullen very well. But I know that in the time he's been here in Last Chance, he's given you and that little boy a good home when he had absolutely nothing to gain from it."

That was true. "But he wasn't truthful–"

"Wasn't he? Did he lie to you about his past?"

"Well...no, but..."

"I'm not going to tell you what to do, Ruby. But I know that people do change. He was a young man that made some foolish choices, and it sounds like he was punished for them. Love changes people and that man loves you, Ruby. He loves Everett."

Ruby furrowed her brows and looked at her hands. *Could he love her?*

"Love is accepting someone for who they are, even at their weakest, without judgment. Do you love him, Ruby?"

Did she? She knew that he made her feel things she'd never felt before. That so many times she was sure he was about to kiss her, and when he didn't she was left with a longing that seemed to go through to her soul. She knew that the thought of losing him was more than she could bear. *Was that love?* Her gaze flew up to meet Lotty's.

"That's what I thought," she smiled warmly. "Go tell him."

Ruby stood and Lotty hugged her tightly.

"I know we haven't known each other very long, but you've been such a good friend, Lotty. Thank you."

"Friendship isn't about how long you know someone, it's about who walks into your life," Lotty replied. She walked Ruby to her buggy and waited until she climbed up into the seat, then waved as Ruby drove away.

On the way home, Ruby thought about what Lotty told her about Cullen being in love with her. Her stomach grew tense and her heart felt heavy. *He didn't know her secret. That would change everything.*

She brought the buggy to a stop at the barn and climbed down. She could see Ben and Cullen looking at something near the waterwheel that powered the sawmill. Her eyes scanned the property for Everett, who was usually not very far from Cullen. Her breath caught in her throat as she spotted his small form slowly making his way across the frozen pond adjacent to the barn. His arms were stretched out in front of him and Ruby could see a small rabbit hopping in front of him, oblivious to the danger of thin spring ice.

"Everett, stop!" she shouted. The boy stopped and turned to look at her at the same time Ruby heard a sickening crack and she watched in horror as Everett disappeared beneath the ice. She ran as fast as she could to the pond, but the hole where Everett fell through was too far for her to reach safely. "Cullen!" she screamed. "Cullen, help!"

Cullen must have seen what happened because he was there before Ruby could call his name again, Ben right on his heels.

"Ben, you stay here, I'll need you to help me back," he ordered and ran onto the ice. There was another loud crack and the hole widened, sucking Cullen down into its darkness.

"No!" Ruby cried and tried to run toward the hole. A strong hand gripped her arm.

"No, Miss Ruby," Ben's urgent voice pleaded

with her. "You can't go in too."

Seconds seemed like hours as she stared at the hole and suddenly Cullen's head popped above the surface. *Where was Everett?* Cullen took a deep breath and disappeared underneath the water once again. Ruby felt like the life was leeching out of her as she waited, barely daring to breathe. *Lord, please be with Cullen and Everett. Guide them to safety...I need them, Lord.* Tears ran freely down her face and she pressed her fist against her mouth to keep from screaming.

Once again Cullen's head broke the surface of the water, and this time she could see he had Everett clutched in his arms. *The boy wasn't moving.* Ruby's heart pounded in her chest as she watched Cullen use his free arm to widen the hole as he worked his way closer to where she and Ben stood. Ben reached a long arm forward and grasped Cullen's hand, pulling him and Everett to safety.

Ruby felt the color drain from her face as Cullen

placed Everett's limp form on the ground and rolled him onto his side. He firmly hit the child between the shoulder blades with the palm of his hand. Nothing happened. He did it again, and a gush of water flowed from Everett's mouth and he began to sputter. Ruby burst into tears and dropped to her knees and cradled the coughing child in her arms.

His lashes fluttered and he looked up at her. "D-did I c-atch the b-b-bunny?"

Ruby let out a short guffaw and pulled him close. "Oh, Everett."

"We need to get him warm," Cullen said through chattering teeth.

Ben pulled Everett from Ruby's arms and ran toward the house. Once inside, he lay Everett on the floor in front of the fireplace.

"Get out of those wet clothes," Ruby ordered Cullen, while she pulled Everett's wet clothes off of him and wrapped him in a blanket. He shook uncontrollably. Cullen came out of the bedroom in dry clothes, his teeth still chattering and his lips an odd shade of blue.

She had to get them warm. She sat Everett on the floor as close to the fire as she dared and grabbed a couple more blankets. Wrapped one around Cullen's shoulders, she guided him to the rocking chair, then wrapped the other around Everett and placed him in Cullen's arms. She poured hot water from a pot on the cook stove into two mugs and had them drink it, silently giving thanks at the same time she prayed for them to be all right.

Several hours later, Everett and Ben played happily with the ark. His fall through the ice all but forgotten. Cullen's lips were no longer blue, and he sat at the table sipping a cup of coffee. Ruby, overcome with the pent up emotion that now wanted to flood through her, went into the bedroom and closed the door. She walked over by the window, covered her face with her hands and silently cried.

The door creaked open and Cullen stepped into

the room. He pulled the door shut behind him and pulled Ruby into his arms. "He's going to be all right," he said. "We can take him into town so Heather can look at him if you want, but I think he's going to be just fine."

Ruby looked up at him through her tears. "I...I thought I lost you both," she cried.

He tucked a stray hair behind her ear. "You aren't going to get rid of me that easily," he said.

"I'm bad luck," she sobbed. "I bring bad luck."

"Ruby, it was an accident," he reached for her but she stepped back.

"You don't understand," her breath hitched. "I prayed for Cyrus not to come back. I prayed something would happen to him so he wouldn't come home. And then they all died," she covered her face and began to sob again.

Cullen pulled her close and kissed the top of her head. "You had nothing to do with that, Ruby. None of that was your fault."

She looked up at him, desperately wanting to believe him. He wiped her tears away with his thumbs.

"Sometimes bad things just happen," he reassured her. "You didn't make it happen."

She lowered her head. *She had to tell him.* Ruby stepped out of his embrace. Her chest was so tight she could barely breathe. "I can't be what you want, Cullen. What you deserve," she sputtered.

He looked at her and shook his head.

"I can't give you children." *There. She'd said it. She couldn't give him the one thing that a wife was supposed to give her husband.*

Cullen cupped her face in his strong, calloused hands. "Let me tell you something, Ruby Parker. *You* are my family. You and Everett. I have everything I need, everything I want, right here. That is, if you'll still have me," he said, his eyes again pleading for her understanding. "I've truly changed, and I'll spend the rest of our lives proving it to you if you let me. I love you, Ruby Parker. I love you just as you are."

She stared into his eyes, and in them saw acceptance and love. She felt a strange flutter in her stomach and her gaze dropped to his lips. She stood on her toes and closed her eyes as she brought her mouth to his. He froze for an instant, but then kissed her back with a passion she didn't know was possible. *Love*, she thought. *This is love.*

Epilogue

June, 1879 – Last Chance, Nebraska

Cullen finished cutting the last board and stretched his back. The sun's position in the sky told him it was nearly time for dinner and he walked to the house. He walked past the garden and smiled at the neat green rows of vegetable plants poking through the dark soil. He thought back to the day they planted the seeds. Ruby kept slipping bean seeds into the holes he'd made for the corn, and then stood at the end of the row and giggled at him. Since she'd proclaimed her love for him, they'd become incredibly close. He hadn't known love like theirs was even possible.

His brother, Ben decided to stay in Last Chance. With Frank gone, he had nowhere else to go. Cullen knew Ben had no desire to continue his criminal life. He'd just been following what Frank did. He'd been doing that his entire life. Cullen and Ruby talked about it, and decided to let Ben have the house and land she shared with Cyrus. The small cabin was perfect for him. Once Ruby had decided to let their past go, she and Ben had become good friends.

"Everett," he called. "Wash up for dinner." The boy was playing near the barn with the puppy he'd gotten for his birthday. The Gruby's dog, Racer, had puppies in late January, and Lotty kept one aside for them. It had been hard waiting until Everett's birthday to give him the pup, but it was the perfect gift for his first real birthday. The little dog was all black with one speck of white on the center of her head, and Everett named her Dot.

Cullen stepped into the house and was surprised to find Ruby sitting at the table, her head on her arms, fast asleep. It was the second time that week that he'd found her asleep at the table. He touched her arm and she slowly woke, groggily wiping her eyes. It seemed to take her a minute to get her bearing and when she did, she jumped to her feet.

"I'm sorry, I didn't mean to fall asleep," she said in a voice that didn't sound at all normal.

Cullen watched the color drain from her face and her eyes roll back in her head as she pitched forward. His arms shot out and caught her before she could fall and he carried her into their bedroom and lay her on the bed. He went back out to get a damp cloth and gently wiped her face with it until her eyes fluttered back open.

"I'm sorry, I don't know what came over me," she struggled to sit but Cullen stilled her. "I'm just so tired."

He could see she was tired. Fatigue painted light purple shadows under her eyes. She'd also been ill, barely eating enough to keep a bird alive. Worry ran through him as he thought about what he should do. *She needed to see the doctor.*

"You rest, I'm going to run into town with Everett and fetch the new doctor," he said.

"No," she protested weakly. "I'll be fine."

Cullen's jaw tightened. "It's not open for discussion, Ruby."

She let out a sigh. "All right, but bring Heather. I don't know the new doctor."

He brushed a hair back from her face and cupped her cheek. He pressed a soft kiss to her lips and straightened. "I'll be back as soon as I can, you just rest awhile."

"Thank you, Cullen. I love you," she said softly as her eyes drifted shut again.

A short time later, Cullen returned with Heather. Ruby was still sleeping and he gently roused her. Heather sent Cullen out of the bedroom so she could examine Ruby.

"Is she going to be all right, Pa?" Everett asked,

worry etched in his small face. There had been no lasting effects from his fall into the pond, but he wouldn't go near it anymore.

"Miss Heather is going to check to make sure," Cullen said.

The minutes slowly ticked by as he waited, anxiously tapping his fingers on the table. Finally, the door opened and Heather motioned for him to come in.

"Can I come too?" Everett asked.

Cullen glanced at Heather, and she nodded. He walked into the bedroom, filled with trepidation. He couldn't stand it if anything was wrong with her and he said a quick prayer. Ruby was sitting on the bed and he stood next to her.

"What's wrong?" Cullen asked. "Will she be all right?"

Heather grinned. "She will. She has morning sickness."

Cullen blinked and glanced at Ruby, who looked

as confused as he did.

"She's going to have a baby," Heather laughed. "It should come right around Christmas, if my guess is right, and it usually is."

Cullen stood unable to move or speak while her words sunk in. *Ruby was pregnant. They were going to have a baby.* He let out a whoop and picked up Ruby, swinging her in a circle. He abruptly stopped and placed her back on her feet. "I'm sorry, I shouldn't have done that," he shot a panicked glance at Heather.

She laughed again. "She's pregnant, Cullen, she's not going to break."

"It wasn't me," Ruby looked up at him, relief washing over her features.

Cullen gave a light shake of his head, not sure what she meant.

"Don't you see?" She gave him a bright smile. "It wasn't me that couldn't have a child, it was Cyrus."

Understanding came over him and he pulled her

close.

"Does that mean I'm going to be a brother?" Everett asked.

"Yes," Cullen and Ruby said in unison as their eyes met.

Everett let out a little whoop and danced a silly little jig with Dot nipping at his heels, sending everyone into peals of laughter. Their little family, already full of love, was growing.

Keep reading for a sneak peek at Laura's other Blizzard Bride book, A Groom for Violet.

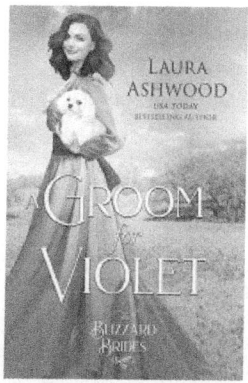

A Note from the Author

While most of A Groom for Ruby takes place in the fictional town of Last Chance, Nebraska, I've included a number of real locations in the story. Dodge City, Kansas, is where we first meet Cullen Parker. The Morgan Gang was inspired by the real-life Dalton Gang, who spent time in Dodge City, among other places. Wyatt Earp and Doc Holliday resided in Dodge City during the time period this story is set as well.

Cullen's past was inspired by Black Bart, the notorious outlaw who did, in fact, do time at San Quentin and wasn't heard from again after his pardon. While I'm not sure what happened to the real Black Bart, my decision to have Cullen travel to the gold mines in South Dakota after his release was inspired by my own family history.

Cullen was on his way to find work at the Homestake Mine in Lead, South Dakota, when he stumbled across Ruby in Last Chance. The Homestake Mine was actually the largest and deepest gold mine in North America until it closed in 2002. One of my uncles worked there for over 15 years. In the summer of 2021, my husband and I made a trip to the Black Hills to attend Wild Deadwood Reads, an annual reader event (if you haven't been, I would highly recommend!) and were able to stop in Lead and visit the Homestake Mine, which is now open for tours. In the front is a set of monuments honoring their employees and after some searching, I was able to locate my uncle's name etched in the granite. It really brought the story even more to life for me.

Leave a Review

Did you enjoy this book? Please consider leaving a review. They can be as long or short as you want and are very much appreciated. Thank you!

Sneak Peek! A Groom for Violet Chapter One:

♥

March 1879

Heaving a sigh of frustration, Violet Stapleton scanned the mercantile for Phyllis Talley one last time before stepping up to the counter where Mr. Talley was busy refilling a large glass container of colorful penny candy.

"Good morning, Mrs. Stapleton," he looked up and the corners of his mouth lifted from under his thick, dark moustache into a toothy grin.

Violet's brows dipped and she glanced over her shoulder, half expecting to see her mother-in-law, Cora, behind her. Heat rose up her face and settled into her cheeks as she realized the man was speaking to her.

She didn't think she'd ever get used to being called Mrs. Stapleton, even though it had been over six months since she had come to Last Chance to marry Wyatt Stapleton.

They'd been married just a week when Wyatt left with most of the town's menfolk on a hunting trip and never returned, victims of a freak early season blizzard. Violet shook off the errant thought and fixed her attention on the man on the other side of the counter.

She watched Mr. Talley place a small silver scoop in the jar, then turn and set it on the shelf behind him next to several other jars filled with various confections. "Your order arrived yesterday," he placed a lid on the jar, then turned back toward her and reached under the counter to retrieve a small paper-wrapped parcel which he set in front of her.

Violet returned his smile and let out a small sigh of relief. "Just in time. Is Mrs. Talley in? I didn't see her."

Mr. Talley shook his head. "She's visiting Mrs. Purcell. I'm not sure when she'll be back," he shrugged. "Is there anything else I can get you?"

Violet's shoulders dropped a bit. She'd been looking forward to going through the Montgomery Ward catalog with Phyllis.

"Yes, I would also like a small bag of white sugar, please." As she waited for Mr. Talley to measure and weigh the sugar, her gaze drifted back to the candy jars.

A wave of nostalgia came over her at the sight of the jar filled with cherry drops. She could almost see her father standing in front of her as a small child, patting the pockets of his frock coat, encouraging her to guess which one contained a treat. She somehow managed to pick the correct pocket every time, and he'd reach in and pull out a lemon or cherry drop for her. Then she'd wrap her arms around him, inhaling the slightly sweet, earthy scent of pipe tobacco that always lingered on his clothes.

"That'll be nineteen cents" Mr. Talley's voice brought her back to the present, and Violet swallowed back the lump that had formed in her throat. She plucked two dimes out of her reticule and handed them to Mr. Talley, and gave another quick glance to the jars of candy. "Can I also get a penny's worth of lemon drops, please?" She smiled, satisfied with her choice.

While she waited for him to get the candy, Violet reached back into her reticule and pulled out a calling card. It still read Violet Montgomery, but she hadn't had a chance to order replacements yet, and it looked like it would have to wait again. She knew Mr. Talley was capable of assisting her, but Violet felt more comfortable ordering such items from Phyllis.

She was still trying to adjust to life in the small town of Last Chance, and hoped Mrs. Talley might be able to help. Last Chance was so different than Charleston, in nearly every way. She folded the upper right corner of the card over, as was custom, and placed it on the counter in front of her.

The bells over the door chimed and Otis Ignatius Graham stumbled into the store. He staggered to the counter next to where Violet waited and leaned on it with both arms. His brown hair was mussed and his clothes were stained and dusty. The sour scent of body odor mixed with alcohol and tobacco filled the space, and Violet hoped Mr. Talley would hurry.

Otis turned to her, one rheumy blue eye focused on her while the other looked off into the distance, and nodded in greeting. Violet gave the man a polite smile in return and slipped her gloves back on her hands. She let out a sigh of relief as Mr. Talley handed her her purchases.

"Thank you, can you please see that Mrs. Talley gets my..." Violet's words turned into a gasp as she watched Otis pick up her calling card and stick it between his teeth in an attempt to fish out some sort of food particle with it. Violet took a step backwards and opened her mouth, but was unable to say anything.

"I'll be sure to let Mrs. Talley know you inquired of her," Mr. Talley said through gritted teeth. "Give my best to the elder Mrs. Stapleton."

Violet's eyes flitted from him to Otis, who was still picking at his teeth with her card. She blinked several times, then slowly nodded her head. "Th-thank you," she managed, forcing a smile, then turned and hurried out of the store.

She made two quick stops. One at the post office to check the mail for Cora, and the other at the bank, before she climbed into the buggy. Settling onto the seat, Violet pulled her wrap tighter around her shoulders in an attempt to ward off the chill that was now seeping into her bones. It had been considerably warmer when she left the Stapleton house. Cora had warned her how quickly spring weather could change, and Violet wished she would have remembered to take the buggy quilt with her.

Squaring her shoulders, she carefully threaded the reins through her fingers like Wyatt had taught her and snapped the reins. She turned the horses onto Scott's Bluff Road and headed west.

Winter in Nebraska was much colder than the winters she'd experienced back home. It seemed as though it was always windy and she'd never experienced anything like the blizzards that killed so many the previous fall. While it was true Charleston did occasionally get blasted by a tropical cyclone, they weren't common like the snow and cold here.

The Stapletons' lived just a few miles west of Last Chance, but the ride home today seemed to take much longer than usual. The wind had loosened the knot in Violet's hair and it whipped violently around her face, while tiny pellets of snow stung like needles. Ice covered the road and forced her to keep the horse moving at a slow trot. A wall of thick, grey clouds replaced the brilliant blue sky from earlier that morning, and created a dreary backdrop for the pillowy white snow drifts.

By the time she reached the Stapletons' farm and brought the buggy to a stop in front of the large whitewashed barn, Violet's fingers were so cold she could no longer feel the reins in her hands. She had no more than brought the horses to a stop when the barn door opened and Eli Stapleton came rushing out to help her down from the seat of the buggy. Her cold feet were unsteady and she was grateful for the assistance.

"Hi, Violet," his whole face spread into a smile as he took the reins from her hands. "I can take care of the horses for you."

Eli was Wyatt's younger brother who, at the tender age of fourteen - make that fifteen today - considered himself the man of the house since Wyatt's death.

"Thank you, Eli," Violet said, and collected her packages from the floor of the buggy.

"It's no trouble," Eli averted his gaze and focused his attention on the horse beside him. Violet watched as a deep red flush she suspected had nothing to do with the cold crept up the boy's neck and colored his cheeks. She suppressed a chuckle and ran stiff-legged toward the house, eager to get out of the cold.

She stepped inside the modest home and was greeted by the delicious aroma of freshly baked bread, and a small, white barking bundle of fur. Violet pulled off her gloves and stooped to pick up the squirming animal.

"Hi Daisy," she cooed in the dog's ear. "I'm sorry my hands are so cold." She tried to stomp her feet to get the snow off her shoes, but they felt like blocks of wood attached to her legs. She hobbled across the room and stood in front of the fireplace, cuddled the dog against her chest, and closed her eyes, trying to will the heat to warm her faster.

"Violet, you're back," said a soft voice from behind her. Violet opened her eyes and turned to face her mother-in-law. She flashed Cora Stapleton a smile, but her cheeks were still numb and she feared it looked like more of a grimace. She was unable to stop her teeth from chattering long enough to say anything.

"Goodness, you're half frozen," the tall, willowy woman lifted the packages out of Violet's stiff fingers and placed them on the table. She then took one of the chairs nestled under the table, dragged it in front of the fireplace, and motioned for Violet to sit down.

Violet complied, got Daisy settled in her lap and wrapped her arms around herself, her teeth chattered together uncontrollably. She couldn't stop herself from shaking.

Cora slipped the damp wrap from Violet's shoulders and shook her head. "Is this all you had on?

Didn't you bring the quilt?" She slid a glance at the wooden box on the floor next to the door where the thick quilt she'd told Violet to bring with her still lay in a neatly folded bundle.

Violet cast her gaze down to her lap. "I f-forgot it," she had trouble getting the words out, her teeth were chattering so hard. Deep down, she knew Cora was simply concerned, but years of her aunt's berating her still played in her head. She couldn't bear the thought she might have done something to disappoint this woman who had done so much for her.

"Well, you can use it now," Cora crossed the room and picked up the quilt, then wrapped it around Violet's shoulders. She pulled a tin cup out of the cupboard, filled it with coffee from the pot on the cook stove, and handed it to Violet.

Violet curled her hands around the warm cup and took a gracious sip of the hot, slightly bitter liquid. Comforting warmth spread through her body, her teeth stopped chattering, the tremors subsided, and she began to relax.

Cora filled a cup for herself, slid another chair close to the fireplace, and settled into it. "Was there any mail today?" she asked.

Violet shook her head and watched the glint of hope in Cora's eyes instantly fade away.

Cora sighed. "Thank you for checking."

A wave of sadness swept over Violet. She wished she knew what Cora was waiting for. If she did, she may be able to help. She chewed her lip, thinking how she might ask without being intrusive. She'd been taught that it wasn't polite to inquire about someone's personal business, but Cora was family. Wasn't that different? Yes, she decided. It was.

"Is there something I might be able to help with?"

Cora hesitated, then let out a deep breath. "Planting season is approaching," she said. "Unless Emmett comes home, Eli is going to have to spend more time in the field. He can't possibly do the planting and all the chores, he's much too young," she wrung her hands in her lap. "He already does so much. I may need your help with some of the barn chores."

Since Violet's arrival at the Stapleton farm, Cora had not been willing to let her do much more than simple household tasks. Of course, it didn't help that she didn't know how to do much more than that. She'd been raised with a series of maids in an environment where ladies were to be waited on, and felt completely inept in this different way of life. She was constantly fearful that at any moment, Cora would ask her to leave. This would give her a chance to prove her worth.

Violet didn't hesitate. "Yes, of course. I would be happy to help. You've done so much for me, it's the least I can do." She had no idea what "barn chores" might consist of, but was willing to help in any way she could.

"Thank you," Cora smiled, relief washing over her features. "Perhaps Emmett will reply soon, there's still time."

Emmett was Wyatt's older brother, but very little had been said about him since her arrival. Violet's knowledge of him consisted of the fact that he made a deposit into Cora's bank account each month, and that he'd been doing so ever since his father's death. Aside from that, she knew nothing about him.

She'd been surprised when he hadn't come home after Wyatt was killed, and even more so knowing that still hadn't returned even after Cora had asked him to. *What kind of son would do that?* She knew all too well that money didn't solve every problem, especially if you were a woman.

Violet's curiosity got the better of her. "Where is Emmett?" she asked.

"He's in Denver," Cora said, but didn't offer any further information.

"You don't speak of him."

Cora gazed at the fireplace with a dull stare, the dancing flames reflected in her eyes, but she remained silent.

"Neither did Wyatt," Violet said in a soft voice. Wyatt told her he had an older brother, but said they didn't speak and made it clear that further conversation about the subject wasn't welcome. There was so much about her husband that Violet didn't know. Didn't get a chance to know.

Cora shifted her gaze to Violet and studied her face. "I just assumed Wyatt had told you," she said, shaking her head. "But it doesn't really surprise me that he didn't."

Violet stroked the soft fur of the sleeping dog in her lap and listened intently.

"Emmett and Wyatt have been rivals ever since they were small children. They were so different, you see? Wyatt was just like his father. He loved the land. He could stand and look out over a field, and it was like it spoke to him in some sort of secret language. Eli is the same way. Nothing makes him happier than being outside, working in the dirt."

"Emmett and William," Cora paused and stared

at the steaming cup grasped between her fingers with a faraway look in her eyes. She brought the cup up to her mouth with a small sigh and took a sip. "Emmett and William, on the other hand, always had their noses in a book."

"William?"

Cora's shoulders drooped. "William was four years younger than Wyatt. He was killed in the same accident that took their father."

Violet inhaled sharply and covered her mouth with her hand. Daisy shifted on her lap, gave a huff of annoyance at the sudden movement of her master, and closed her eyes.

"Even though Emmett had left by then, Wyatt blamed him for the accident. Said if he'd been there, it never would have happened."

"Is that true?"

Cora shook her head sadly. "No. It was an accident. If it hadn't been William, it would have been Emmett."

Violet leaned forward, careful this time not to disturb the sleeping dog. "What happened?"

"Ernest was cutting down trees in the hollow down by the creek. There were several big oak trees he wanted to fell, but he needed help. Wyatt was in the field, and Eli was far too young, so he took William with him. I told Ernest to wait until Wyatt could help. William was not good with the horses, and not nearly as strong as Wyatt," she explained. "But he wanted to get them down before the snow came."

Violet's heart ached for the tragedy this woman, this family had endured. She was no stranger to what it was like to lose someone close, but this woman had not only lost her husband, but two of her children. She reached over and grasped Cora's hand, giving it a gentle squeeze. "When did this happen?"

Cora's brows furrowed a moment. "It was five years last fall." She returned the squeeze and placed her other hand on top of their joined hands, then continued. "They were trying to pull a large log up the side of the hill. It had rained the day before and the ground was damp. The horse slipped and the chain snapped," she trailed off, closing her eyes. A tear ran down one cheek and disappeared under the collar of her dress. She cleared her throat and continued.

"The chain hit William in the head, and Ernest didn't have time to get out of the way. By the time we realized something was wrong, Ernest was gone. William hung on for a few hours, but his injury was too severe to overcome."

They sat in silence for several minutes. How awful that must have been for Cora. Violet's thoughts filtered back to her Aunt Dorcas telling her that her parents weren't coming back. A shiver ran down her spine. *No! She was not going to allow herself to think about that day.* She swallowed down the lump in her throat and gave Cora's hand another squeeze. "I'm so sorry," she said.

Cora glanced at the clock on the mantle and

jumped to her feet. "Oh my goodness, I didn't realize it was so late. I need to get the cake made."

Daisy, startled by the movement, let out a yip of displeasure and Violet gently placed her on her cushion near the fireplace hearth, where she promptly curled up and went back to sleep.

Violet stood. "Let me help you," she followed Cora to the cabinet and watched as she pulled out a large bowl and placed it on the table. Violet reached for the package of sugar and handed it to her. "I brought some white sugar for the cake," she grinned.

"Violet, you shouldn't spend your money on such frivolous things," Cora half-heartedly chided as she reached for the bag, unable to hide the smile in her voice.

"*Birthday cakes should always be sweetened with white sugar*, is what my m-mother . . ." Violet stumbled over the word, the lump in her throat threatening to return. She swallowed it back down and continued, "always said."

She reached for the package containing the order Mr. Talley had given her and unwrapped it. Fifteen small, narrow candles lay nestled in the paper. "And they should always have candles."

"Eli has never had such a birthday treat," excitement flashed in Cora's eyes. She quickly measured ingredients into the bowl and made a thick batter.

It never ceased to amaze Violet how mixing together items that would be inedible on their own, could magically turn them into any number of delicious dishes. Their cook back in Charleston was competent, but couldn't hold a candle to Cora Stapleton. Violet wondered if she would ever master the skill. She would inevitably leave out an ingredient, or over or undercook whatever it was she was attempting to make.

Violet watched Cora expertly pour the cake batter into a cast iron skillet and made a mental note to order her one of the special cake baking pans she'd seen her old cook use next time she was at the mercantile.

"I can make whipped cream for on top of the cake," Violet offered. *Surely she couldn't mess that up.*

Cora hesitated just long enough to make Violet wish she hadn't asked. She had ruined a number of dishes since her arrival because of her incompetence. But to her surprise, Cora agreed.

Violet carefully poured the cream into a bowl and added a touch of the white sugar, just as she'd seen Cora do many times before. Then, using a whisk, whipped the cream as fast as she could.

The muscles in her arm were screaming by the time stiff peaks began to form in the bowl, and Violet was determined to make them as high as possible. But instead of getting taller, she watched in horror as they started to shrink. Violet switched arms and whipped harder, but the faster she went, the lower the peaks went and the thicker the cream became. Defeated, she removed the whisk from the bowl and turned to Cora.

"What have I done wrong?" she frowned.

Cora glanced into the bowl and started laughing. "You've made butter."

Get a free book! Sign up for Laura's newsletter and get Snowflakes & Second Chances, a subscriber exclusive novella, for free!

About Laura

Laura Ashwood is a USA Today Bestselling author of sweet contemporary and historical western romance, and women's fiction.

In her novels, Laura brings to life characters and relationships that will warm your heart and fill you with hope. Her stories often have themes involving redemption, forgiveness, and family.

Laura and her husband live in northeast Minnesota, which is the setting for many of her stories. She has a full time day job as an executive administrative assistant, and in her spare time, she likes to read, cook and spend time with her husband. She is a devoted grandmother and chihuahua lover.

She is a member of American Christian Fiction Writers (ACFW) and Women's Fiction Writers of America (WFWA).

Find her on Facebook, Bookbub, Instagram, Pinterest, Twitter, and Goodreads. Go to www.lauraashwood.com to see all her books.

If you liked this book, please take a minute to leave a review for it. Authors (Laura included) really appreciate this, and it helps draw more readers to books they might like. Thank you!

Made in the USA
Monee, IL
09 January 2026

41274019R00152